Praise for Dorothy Gilman, Mrs. Pollifax, and MRS. POLLIFAX PURSUED

"Mrs. Pollifax already has picked up a legion of followers who will find . . . an entertaining blend of humor, suspense, and charm."

—*The Charlotte Observer*

"Rejoice, mystery fans . . . [Gilman's] flair for suspense and globetrotting excitement should move MRS. POLLIFAX PURSUED to the top of every mystery lover's 'must read' list!"

—*Mostly Murder*

"MRS. POLLIFAX PURSUED is another fine entry in this popular series. The carnival setting is fascinating and the story has a nice, surprising ending."

—*Romantic Times*

"Filled with adventures—and misadventures—but through it all, Mrs. Pollifax is triumphant."

—*Booklist*

"Utterly delightful."

—*The Pittsburgh Press*

By Dorothy Gilman
Published by Fawcett Books:

UNCERTAIN VOYAGE
A NUN IN THE CLOSET
THE CLAIRVOYANT COUNTESS
THE TIGHTROPE WALKER
INCIDENT AT BADAMYÂ
CARAVAN
THE BELLS OF FREEDOM
THE MAZE IN THE HEART OF THE CASTLE
GIRL IN BUCKSKIN
THALE'S FOLLY
KALEIDOSCOPE

The Mrs. Pollifax series
THE UNEXPECTED MRS. POLLIFAX
THE AMAZING MRS. POLLIFAX
THE ELUSIVE MRS. POLLIFAX
A PALM FOR MRS. POLLIFAX
MRS. POLLIFAX ON SAFARI
MRS. POLLIFAX ON THE CHINA STATION
MRS. POLLIFAX AND THE HONG KONG BUDDHA
MRS. POLLIFAX AND THE GOLDEN TRIANGLE
MRS. POLLIFAX AND THE WHIRLING DERVISH
MRS. POLLIFAX AND THE SECOND THIEF
MRS. POLLIFAX PURSUED
MRS. POLLIFAX AND THE LION KILLER
MRS. POLLIFAX, INNOCENT TOURIST
MRS. POLLIFAX UNVEILED

Nonfiction
A NEW KIND OF COUNTRY

MRS. POLLIFAX PURSUED

Dorothy Gilman

FAWCETT

BALLANTINE BOOKS • NEW YORK

A Fawcett Book
Published by The Random House Publishing Group

Published in the United States by Fawcett Books, an imprint of The Random House Publishing Group, a division of Random House, Inc., New York, and simultaneously in Canada by Random House of Canada Limited, Toronto.

FAWCETT is a registered trademark and the Fawcett colophon is a trademark of Random House, Inc.

ISBN 978-0-449-14956-0

Printed in the United States of America

www.ballantinebooks.com

First Hardcover Edition: February 1995
First Mass Market Edition: January 1996

M 19 18

PROLOGUE

HENRY BIDWELL WAS RICH BUT THIS WAS of little consequence to him since he had always been rich. What mattered most to him was that he was successful in his work, his wealth increasing each day as a result of his own clear thinking, acute judgments, and calculations. He held a vital position in Claiborne-Osborne International, a conservative investment and holding company that prided itself on its global connections and was dedicated to making even more money smoothly, discreetly, and with well-concealed ruthlessness. He traveled abroad frequently to inspect these varied interests and to investigate new acquisitions, moving in a world made seamless by ease and convenience.

On this late Friday afternoon in April before departing from his desk he checked his calendar, noted that his wife was entertaining a dozen people for dinner that evening, and that he could anticipate a weekend of golf. As he nodded with satisfaction his phone rang and he frowned. His secretary had already left for the day and he did not appreciate phones that rang without Miss Ferguson's intervention. Nevertheless he picked up the receiver, said sharply, "Bidwell here," and listened to the voice at the other end, murmured, "I understand . . . you can't tell me when?" And then, "Of course, yes," and hung up. Following a glance at his gold Breitling watch he brushed a speck of lint from his Armani suit and picked up his briefcase, knowing that his chauffeur, Georges, would arrive punctually in five minutes. Walking to his private elevator he descended eighteen floors to the lobby, made his exit through the bank of glass doors, and walked out into the pleasant late afternoon sunlight. His limousine had not yet pulled into the NO PARKING space opposite the lobby doors; at the moment the space had been usurped by a dirty white van with a misspelled CHIGI SCAP METAL painted on its panel.

The driver of the van, giving him a sharp glance, looked a cheeky fellow in a ragged cap; his confederate had just walked around the van to its rear and was unlocking and opening the two rear doors. Bidwell stepped to the edge of the sidewalk and said sternly, "Look here, my good man, you can't stop here. Can't you read? No parking allowed."

The man gave him a mocking glance and said scornfully, "Put your head in a bucket, mister."

"The law is very strict," pointed out Mr. Bidwell. "On this street especially, the police—"

The man narrowed his eyes and moved toward him aggressively. "Yeah?"

Bidwell retreated a step from the curb but the man followed, thrusting his face close to Bidwell's. "Yeah?" he repeated, and lifted a dirty hand to shake a filthy rag in Bidwell's face.

It was at this moment that Bidwell realized he had misunderstood the situation, that this confrontation had been planned, it was premeditated, because something was certainly wrong: the rag shoved into his face had been saturated with a chemical both unpleasant and penetrating, and his quick gasp only made worse the fumes searing his nostrils and throat. He was aware of the sidewalk beginning to move giddily up and down in front of him, ultimately coiling like a snake and then blurring fuzzily. As Mr. Bidwell slid down to join it hc felt himself caught, lifted, carried away, and dumped on a hard metal surface. When the door slammed he was already unconscious on the floor of the Chigi Scrap Metal van.

CHAPTER 1

MRS. POLLIFAX, RELAXING FOR A FEW minutes over coffee at her kitchen table, dutifully scanned the headlines of the morning newspaper: OPEC MEETING ABORTIVE; FOOD RIOTS IN UBANGIBA; TORNADO HITS KANSAS; but she was far more interested in the abduction of Henry Bidwell six days ago, about which there was a long article, but with very little fresh news. His disappearance intrigued her; she enjoyed mysteries, having been involved in a number of them herself. Words like *snatched* appealed to her, and *no witnesses*—on such a busy street, too—fueled her curiosity. Reading further she discovered that "no witnesses" was not quite true: the police had now unearthed a fruit vendor on the next block who had noticed Bidwell standing on the curb because he'd seen him sway dizzily and be helped into a car. *Taken sick,* the vendor had thought, but since his view had been blocked by lines of parked cars, and he had been half a block away, his information was too scanty to be of help. Bidwell, however, remained missing and it was becoming more and more obvious that because of his position he'd been abducted for ransom.

If his situation intrigued Mrs. Pollifax, his importance did not, since planting basil in her greenhouse was the more vital to her this morning. Draining her cup of coffee, she picked up her trowel and walked through the open door into the bright sunny greenhouse. Her geraniums were blossoming in colorful profusion but this year she was planting herbs, too, and she noted that both the mints and the sage were nearly ready to be transplanted into the garden. *This* was where she celebrated spring, planting and nurturing, adjusting vents and shade and drinking in the pungent smells of warm earth, lime, bone meal, and mint.

Glancing up from her work she was surprised to see a shabby white van once again drive past the house on its way up Maple Lane. She frowned because she had seen it pass the house three times yesterday, noticing it especially because of the sign on its side panel, which she had mentioned to Cyrus as he packed to attend the meeting of the American Bar Association.

"Lost art, spelling," he'd said. "Emily, where's the other blue tie I wear with this shirt?"

"You'll only be away until Monday," she'd reminded him.

"I spill," he pointed out. "Bound to spill if I don't carry spares."

She had laughed and restored the extra ties to his suitcase, but later the van had driven past for the third time and she had noticed how it slowed at the sight of Cyrus checking the tires of the car in the driveway. It was impossible to mistake it because it bore the same misspelled sign: CHIGI SCAP METAL.

Now it was passing the house again.

This, she told herself sternly, *is what comes of working for Carstairs and the Department; the antenna keeps working, there is too MUCH awareness, which is all very well on assignments fraught with danger but I am NOT on assignment, I'm in my own house and trying to plant basil.*

On the other hand, she reflected thoughtfully, very few cars used Maple Lane; it was a shortcut to the highway that only neighbors used, and few people knew about, and its usual traffic was familiar to her: Mr. Gogan off to work each morning and returning; Mrs. Haycock driving to her job at the hospital; the young Abners delivering their son to day care, the mail truck, the carpenters building an addition at the Witkowskis.

She supposed that eventually there would be a reasonable explanation for this new vehicle going up and down the lane at such odd hours. What she did not understand was why its frequent appearances had begun to make her uneasy. *I need food,* she decided;

of course she needed food after such an early breakfast, and with a glance at her wrist watch she put aside her trowel and returned to the kitchen. Opening the refrigerator door she inspected its contents critically: the chicken was for dinner, the salad—but she didn't want salad, she was too hungry after driving Cyrus to the airport at dawn. Her eyes fell on the package of Cyrus's favorite salami, and—*living dangerously*, she thought with a smile—she opened a fresh loaf of bread, unwrapped the salami, and made a sandwich. Pouring a glass of milk she carried her lunch on a tray to the patio where she could sit in the sun and admire the tulips and crocuses.

It was a pleasant scene; beyond the beds of flowers, at a distance, marched a row of birches that lined the unpaved road into the woods, but as her gaze moved from the tulips to the distant trees she saw that she was not as private as she had hoped: something white caught her eye. A car was parked on one side of the woods road, no doubt its occupant eating his or her lunch, too, she thought, and wondered why the discovery made her uncomfortable. With a sigh she stood up and carried her tray back into the house. Depositing it on the dining table, and scolding herself for doing this, she drew out Cyrus's bird-watching binoculars from the drawer of the buffet and walked to the window.

I'm being ridiculous, she thought.

They were very fine binoculars and, although a tree concealed the front of the car and its occupant, she could see that it was a shabby white van and she could make out five letters of the sign on the panel: SCAP M.

"I think," said Mrs. Pollifax aloud, very firmly, "that I will move the car out of the driveway and into the garage."

She had no idea why this was important, and as she walked out of the house and climbed into the car she asked herself why. *Because Cyrus is away?* she wondered, *and I'm alone here? But why move the car?*

Finding no ready answer she drove the car to the rear of the house; the garage doors obediently swung open and closed behind her, and for that moment she felt snug and relaxed. Reentering the house from the garage she walked down the hall past the living room and through the kitchen, and as she reached the greenhouse saw the white van drive past the house and disappear.

She sighed with relief.

Emily, she thought, *you've behaved very irrationally this past hour, and need I remind you that this is the route to paranoia?* With grim resolve she resumed her planting of basil and presently found other matters to think about: the Garden Club meeting tomorrow, for instance, and the sandwiches she had volunteered that were already made and covered with a damp cloth in the refrigerator. Wondering if the men attending the meeting would be content with cucumber sandwiches, it occurred to her that she might add half a dozen sandwiches of salami. *Cholesterol be damned,* she thought, and abandoning the basil she walked into the kitchen to expand the refreshment menu.

The salami, however, was not in the refrigerator. This seemed odd, since she had made a sandwich of it scarcely an hour ago; nevertheless the salami was not where it should have been in the refrigerator, nor was it on the counter or the kitchen table.

Puzzled, she emptied the refrigerator's top shelf of chicken, bread, salad, the platter of Garden Club sandwiches, and a carton of eggs, but the salami had not been hiding behind any of them; it was simply not there. With a sigh of exasperation she began the tiresome job of returning the food to the top shelf, but when she picked up the newly opened loaf of bread it struck her as surprisingly light; she examined it more carefully and felt a vague sense of disquiet because earlier she had extracted two slices from the top of the loaf and now there were at least five slices missing, as well as the crust.

Definitely uneasy now, Mrs. Pollifax walked to the cupboard in which she stored canned goods and ran a sharp eye over its contents. There had been eight tins of sardines yesterday and Cyrus had packed two of them for snacks; there should have been six left but there was now only one. Gone, too, were the screw-top jars of herring, and the six-pack of colas had been reduced to four.

The house suddenly felt oppressively silent. Mrs. Pollifax was no longer uneasy; a small chill was racing down her spine.

What this means, she thought, feeling her way gingerly toward an explanation, *is that while I drove Cyrus to the airport this morning someone broke into this house and stole some food.*

This was the rationale that she preferred, but of course it was entirely wrong because only an hour ago she had made a sandwich of the missing salami and bread.

Very reluctantly she approached the only viable explanation, and she did not like it at all. It meant that she was not alone here, there was someone else in this house with her. Now, at this moment. Hiding somewhere.

CHAPTER 2

MRS. POLLIFAX STOOD VERY STILL, LISTENING, her senses heightened by the knowledge that someone else shared this silence that until a moment ago had been friendly and companionable and had now become threatening. Carefully she took stock of her resources: a flashlight for dark closets, the poker from the fireplace, and her training in karate. She dismissed the thought of calling the police because her call might be overheard in this silent house and bring the intruder out of hiding to confront her on his terms, not hers. *Too risky,* she thought, and armed with poker and flashlight she tiptoed up the stairs to begin at the top of the house.

Closets were opened in the master bedroom, in

Cyrus's study, the guest room, and the hall. Mounting a ladder she slid open the hatch to the attic crawl space and shone her flashlight into each dark corner but found no one. Puzzled, she tiptoed down the stairs to continue her search but here too the closets yielded no one, and she was about to give up and call the police when she remembered the storage closet at the end of the hall next door to the garage, the repository of every miscalculated or outgrown object in the house. He had to be there, she realized, he had to be . . . Approaching it she hesitated, drew a deep breath, and flung open the door.

Her flashlight shone on the old lawn mower, Cyrus's ancient trunk, a wicker birdcage, a pile of old draperies . . . and four empty tins of sardines.

"Oh please," whispered a frightened voice.

Mrs. Pollifax swung her flashlight toward the far corner, and the light shone on a girl huddled there staring at her with frightened eyes. "Please," she whispered again, shielding her eyes against the light.

Not an armed burglar . . . Mrs. Pollifax drew a deep breath and said, "What on earth . . . I mean what on earth are you *doing* here? In my *house*?"

"H-hiding," stammered the girl.

"Obviously," said Mrs. Pollifax dryly, "but who are you? You'd better come out and tell me what this is all about."

The girl shook her head. "Please, not yet, they might see me."

"See you? Who?"

She said, "When you left for the airport this morning—"

"Airport?" repeated Mrs. Pollifax, startled. "You were here this morning? *How long have you been hiding in this closet?*"

"T-two days, I think," the girl stammered. "At least it was Monday, you and your husband were both working in the garden and you'd left the side door open and so—I'm sorry—I just came in."

"All that time!" said Mrs. Pollifax in astonishment. "But who are you hiding from, parents? Police?"

"*Them,*" the girl said. "After you left for the airport this morning I heard a car drive in, I could hear the crunch of gravel. I think they looked in all the windows."

A car . . . the girl was afraid of a car . . . "Come out," Mrs. Pollifax said firmly. "It's quite tiresome standing here talking into a closet and there's no window here in this hallway. I want to know if this has anything to do with a rather dirty white van with a sign Chigi Scap—"

"You've seen it?" gasped the girl. "It's still here? They're still watching? How did you know?"

Mrs. Pollifax said calmly, "Because I watched it pass the house three times yesterday and again this morning, and while I was out on the patio—during which time you removed the salami and bread—it was parked on the road into the woods."

The girl stared at her in surprise. "You notice things like that?"

Mrs. Pollifax smiled. "Definitely I do, yes, and now you will please come out of this closet."

The girl eyed her uncertainly, but she stiffly untangled herself and rose to her feet to climb over the birdcage and make her exit. Once in the hall Mrs. Pollifax looked her over frankly and with some surprise: the girl was smaller than she'd expected, only a shade over five feet in height, with a small pale face and disproportionately large eyes, a rounded chin, and brown hair cut very straight at her shoulder. *Not very prepossessing,* thought Mrs. Pollifax, noting the shabby tweed jacket, wrinkled skirt and stockings, yet the way she squared her shoulders and lifted a defiant chin showed courage, and the intelligence in her eyes suggested maturity: this was not a child but a young woman. In the light of the hallway her eyes looked green, and heavily lashed—really quite lovely in that small face—with dark brows arched like commas above them. She wore no make-up, in fact she didn't look at all like the young girls Mrs. Pollifax saw in the shopping malls; there was something old-fashioned and waiflike about her.

Puzzled, she said, "If you're in danger I think we really must call the police."

"Please no," the girl said earnestly. "If that happens they'll harm Sammy, I know they will. If I could stay until it's dark, I'll go, I promise."

Mrs. Pollifax considered her thoughtfully. "You say you heard a car drive in this morning and the gravel crunching. Did they—whoever they are—try to get into the house?"

She shook her head. "I don't think so, but I could hear footsteps and it was about ten minutes before the gravel crunched again when they drove out. I had the feeling they were looking in all the windows. They couldn't have known how long you'd be away. You were gone a long time, it scared me."

Mrs. Pollifax nodded. "My husband's suitcase went into the trunk of the car last night, when it was dark and the car parked outside. I don't suppose they would have known I was taking him to the airport, they wouldn't have seen the luggage." She added thoughtfully, "But if they were watching the house this morning they would have seen two of us leave and only one return."

The girl's eyes widened. "You mean there are just the two of us now?"

"Yes. Do they know—absolutely—that you're here?"

"Probably," she said in a depressed voice. "Here or in the woods, but they've probably searched the woods. They saw me run into your garden, but you were both outside, so—so they didn't follow."

"I see," said Mrs. Pollifax, nodding, and added crisply, "Then of course they'll want to search the house and I really think we must give them every opportunity to do so while it's daylight because I should object very much to their breaking in at night. Yes, definitely we must encourage them to do it now."

"I don't understand," faltered the girl, "you'll let them find me?"

"Of course not. What I mean," explained Mrs. Pollifax, "is that you and I will both leave the house now and you'll come shopping with me for groceries. Well-hidden in the car, needless to say. The car is in the garage"—*thank heaven,* she thought—"and if I leave very publicly they ought to find it a perfect time to pick locks, enter, and look for you. And when it's dark I'll drive you—" She looked at the girl questioningly. "Drive you home? Or somewhere."

The girl flushed. "You're going to a great deal of trouble for me. I'm sorry. But how can you know if they've searched the house when we get back?"

There was a twinkle in Mrs. Pollifax's eye. "You might say that I am not a stranger to the criminal mind," she told her. "Just leave it to me. Now go and wash your face, you must already know there's a bathroom next to this closet. Wait for me in the hall."

While the girl was in the bathroom, Mrs. Pollifax busied herself inserting tiny slips of sticky tape to the door frames of the front and patio doors, after which she moved vases and pots of flowers to each windowsill downstairs, marking with a pencil precisely where she had placed them. They moved into the garage where Mrs. Pollifax arranged her on the floor of the car with a blanket over her, and then artfully tossed a few empty cardboard cartons on top of her. Backing out of the garage she drove around to the front driveway and stopped by the front door. From this vantage point she made a great show of bringing out her grocery cart and inserting it into the back. She then locked the front door and drove up Maple Lane, where one quick glance told her the white van was parked on the woods road. From here she drove into town to the grocery store.

She was not followed. Parking at the supermarket she said over her shoulder, "No Chigi Scap Metal behind us, I'm locking the car, are you all right?" Hearing a muffled affirmative she added, "I won't be long."

She had shopped only two days ago and needed very little, but at the delicatessen counter she purchased several sandwiches and a bag of cookies for the girl. She was gone only ten minutes, scarcely long enough for a thorough search of her house, and so she continued on to the bank where she cashed a check. Following this she estimated that by the time she reached home she would have given Chigi Scap Metal thirty minutes and she saw no point in lingering. She realized, with some amusement, that anyone else would be appalled at her believing what a nameless girl had told her; anyone else would delight in pointing out to her that the child might be a front for an organized gang of thieves and that she would arrive home to find the house robbed of everything valuable. Anyone else would . . .

Mrs. Pollifax, however, was trusting her instincts, and since they had kept her alive in many a dangerous situation in some very exotic countries, she was not about to abandon them on home territory. Something was wrong and she was determined to find out what it was and who Sammy might be. After all, it had proven a rather dull winter, and a girl in trouble appealed far more to her sense of adventure than a Garden Club meeting.

The garage door opened soundlessly, she drove in, and the door closed behind them. "Wait here—don't move!" she told the girl, and entered the house with a feeling of intense curiosity and a great deal of hope that her scheme had worked.

She was pleased to find the cellophane strips at the front door broken, and proceeded to search the house again. Nothing had been taken. When she returned to the garage she said in a low voice, "You can come out now, they've been in the house and satisfied their curiosity."

"They actually came in?" gasped the girl, pushing aside blankets and cartons and climbing out. "Just as you predicted?"

"Yes, and now I think it's time you introduce yourself. After that I'll scramble some eggs for you and you can tell me where to drive you once it's dark. Where you live."

"The scrambled eggs sound lovely. My name is Kadi Hopkirk, and—"

"Katie?"

She shook her head. "No, K-a-d-i—and I have a room at the YWCA in Manhattan where I go to art school."

"I see . . . and I'm Emily Pollifax. I suggest you

crawl under the windows, and sit on the floor in the kitchen, keeping well out of sight, while I scramble the eggs . . . Chigi Scap Metal *must* have given up by now, but I feel it unwise to assume anything."

"Oh you do understand," the girl said eagerly. "Thank you."

Once ensconced in the kitchen Mrs. Pollifax pursued her inquiries as tactfully as possible. Breaking eggs into a bowl and whipping them she asked, "Were you followed *out* of New York City on Monday, or did this happen after you reached Connecticut?"

"I was in New Haven," explained Kadi. "I heard through the grapevine at school the New Haven police were looking for a quick-sketch artist, and I'm awfully good at remembering faces and drawing likenesses fast. It seems to be what I do best. And I need money. But they thought I was too young," she said with a sigh. "They said I might have to draw corpses—as if I haven't seen enough of them already."

"Oh?" said Mrs. Pollifax with interest, turning to look at her. "*Many* corpses?"

The girl said without expression, "Where I come from there have been—well, massacres, really, so I know what killed people look like."

"I see," said Mrs. Pollifax, and presented her with a platter of eggs. She did not ask the obvious question as to where that might be but she was determined to find out; there would be the long drive into

Manhattan, and once the girl felt safer she would be less tense and guarded.

As she turned away from the girl, however, tray in hand, she glanced through the open greenhouse door and saw the white van pass the house again. *Blast them,* she thought indignantly, *they've searched the house, why are they still haunting Maple Lane?*

She did not mention the reappearance of the van but looked instead at her wrist watch; it was two hours until darkness. Leaving the girl to her lunch she went off to hunt out her road maps and to trace the fastest route into Manhattan.

They left at seven, with Kadi in the back, but unblanketed, lying instead across the rear seat, her head cushioned and low. Mrs. Pollifax took care not to turn on the car's headlights until she had left the driveway behind, and turning left to avoid the woods road she took the shortcut to I-95 south. Traffic was surprisingly light at this hour. Once on the turnpike, aware that Chigi Scap Metal had not yet abandoned Maple Lane, she checked her rearview mirror occasionally while she considered how best to wring from her companion an explanation of what terrified her.

She had driven only seven or eight miles when it became impossible to overlook a dull green sedan at some distance behind them. She noticed it because no matter how many trucks or cars passed her, the sedan remained steadily there, keeping to the same 50 m.p.h. which she was driving. *Coincidence,* she told herself—after all, it was not a white van—but to reassure herself she lightened her foot on the accelerator and gradually slowed until the speedometer needle hovered around 30 m.p.h.

The driver of the green sedan did not pass, however; he, too, slowed to 30 m.p.h.

I don't believe this, thought Mrs. Pollifax in astonishment, *this is not only incredible but very tiresome.* Worse, she realized this implied Chigi Scap Metal's having more resources than expected if they could also produce a green sedan. *If,* of course, it was following them. Seeing an exit sign ahead, and determined to find out, she turned off I-95 and drove down the exit ramp onto a secondary road illumined by the lights of a gas station. She headed into its bright lights and stopped, waiting, her eyes on the rearview mirror.

"What's wrong?" called Kadi from the rear.

"What's wrong," said Mrs. Pollifax grimly, "is that I slowed to a miserable thirty miles per hour and the car behind us *still* didn't pass, except now it's a green sedan, in which case—" She nodded as the dark green car drove down the exit ramp, and pressing her foot hard on the accelerator, tires screaming in outrage, she swerved out of the gas station and headed for the I-95 north ramp, reversing their direction.

"In which case what?" called Kadi.

"In which case we're being followed and I'm heading back north to try and lose them." And to her companion, "Why, Kadi? Who *are* these people?"

"I don't know, I don't know," cried Kadi. "You have to believe me, I don't *know*."

CHAPTER 3

CARSTAIRS WAS EXPERIENCING AN UNusually busy Wednesday when Bishop walked into his office and interrupted him. Carstairs gave him a baleful glance and growled, "Now what?"

"Mornajay's called from Upstairs," Bishop told him. "It's about the Bidwell abduction, the FBI's asked our help in a small matter."

"Like what?"

"Bidwell traveled abroad so often on business that for the moment they're working on the theory that some terrorist group or other in one of those countries might be involved in the kidnapping." He handed Carstairs two sheets of paper and a leather notebook. "He could have made enemies."

Carstairs leaned back in his chair. "They've had a ransom note?"

Bishop nodded. "Yes, but they're keeping it under wraps. It included a rather dim photo of a man bound and gagged whom they've identified as Bidwell, even with his face partially covered."

"Where was the ransom note posted?"

"Manhattan. A postbox near where they seized him but postmarked three days later."

"So what does the FBI want from us they don't already have?"

Bishop said dryly, "The security of certainty, I'd guess . . . the odd chance that we might have one of these names in *our* files. Bidwell's company supplied the dates of each trip he made to Europe. It was Bidwell's secretary who proved a godsend; when they interviewed her she wondered if his personal engagement calendar might still be locked in the drawer of his desk. They picked the lock and have a record in detail of his appointments in Europe. Jed Addams at the FBI is asking us to run these names through our cross-reference files and see if we've picked up any information they don't have."

Carstairs shrugged. "Fair enough." He placed the package to one side with his other paperwork, at which point Bishop said tactfully, "They want it today."

Carstairs groaned. "Then preserve my sanity by bringing me a fresh cup of coffee, will you?"

"Coffee and a hair shirt coming up," said Bishop

cheerfully, and presently placed a cup of steaming coffee on the desk.

Coffee in hand, Carstairs glanced quickly over the dates of travel supplied by Claiborne-Osborne International, and then turned to the more interesting private engagement book that had been locked in the man's desk. Making a note of the many dates when Bidwell had left for Europe, Carstairs turned to those pages in the engagement book to check the people he might have seen, and what projects he'd inspected.

This was now late April. In December Bidwell had flown to Paris and met with a Yule Romanovitch and an Achille Lecler, after which the three had joined a group from the Abercrombie Tin Company and spent the evening at a nightclub. There were various phone numbers scribbled on the pages but Carstairs assumed these had already been checked by the FBI. On Bidwell's second day in Paris he'd had an appointment with Lecler but also with a Rogere Desforges, followed by phone numbers and "flight 1192." The next three pages were blank. On the sixth day he was back in Paris to return to New York on the Concorde.

Three weeks later, still in December, he'd made another trip abroad, this time for a brief stop in Switzerland and then on to Paris for a number of appointments, and on the fifth day the scribbled numbers 1192 appeared again. Curious, Carstairs skipped ahead to the next trip abroad; this had occurred in mid-January, a flight to Paris and again the notation "flight 1192" followed by four blank pages. On

March 3rd he'd flown to Paris, and again in early April, and on each of these trips his calendar included "flight 1192," with pages left blank for several days, before appointments resumed in Paris until his return to the United States. And of course he'd been abducted two weeks later.

The FBI, however, wanted names checked, and these Carstairs proceeded to list: Achille Lecler, Rogere Desforges, Yule Romanovitch, E. Buttersworth, J. Kriveleva, M. Teek Soo . . . He ran these through both computers and then their cross-reference files on terrorist groups, and came up with nothing suspicious about any of the men; they simply weren't listed as dangerous in any respect. They weren't listed at all. Straightforward businessmen, he guessed, and put in a call to Jed Addams at the FBI. "We've nothing on any of them," he told him.

"Damn," said Addams.

"Since we're on the subject of Bidwell," put in Carstairs pleasantly, "what personal life did he happen to have? His marriage? Children?"

Addams said wearily, "No real personal life. His marriage? Seems to have been money marrying money. So-so, if you know what I mean. Two children in Ivy League colleges. His wife plays bridge and gives dinner parties. All image, you know how it is. Affairs? Not Bidwell, he's all business. Only recreation golf."

"You'd say his life is an open book then," concluded Carstairs.

"Well, if you insist on clichés, old chap, yes."

Carstairs frowned as he ended the phone call. They seemed to have missed or ignored the references to a flight 1192, it was names they were interested in. . . . People. As Bishop walked into his office he said absently, "I've reported to the FBI that we've nothing on any of Bidwell's acquaintances in Paris, apparently they all have clean hands and a clean heart."

Bishop nodded. "Sounded a bit crazy to me, anyway. Or desperate."

"But thorough," Carstairs reminded him. "There's one inquiry I'd like you to make for me personally, however, strictly private."

"What's that?"

Carstairs sighed. "My insatiable curiosity, Bishop. On each trip Bidwell made abroad there's a scribbled notation in his engagement book that reads 'flight 1192,' followed by three or four blank pages. See if you can find out from Paris where flight 1192 goes, will you?"

"Right. What airline?"

Carstairs said sheepishly, "None listed."

Startled, Bishop said, "Good God, that's like looking for a needle in a haystack. Two airports in Paris, and how many flights a day?"

"Hundreds. But how many flights 1192?"

Bishop sighed. "Could take a couple of days."

"I'm not only curious, Bishop, but I'm patient. See what you can do."

Bishop said suspiciously, "Does this have anything to do with Bidwell's abduction?"

"Absolutely nothing at all," Carstairs assured him cheerfully.

The inquiry did not take days, however; by early evening Bishop was in his office beaming triumphantly. "Got it! Thank God for computers, Paris has found the needle in the haystack for you."

By now Carstairs had almost forgotten the attack of curiosity that had overtaken him in an earlier season of the day, but the word Paris rallied his memory. "Flight 1192?"

Bishop nodded. "Flight 1192 leaves Paris twice a week for Africa. To Ubangiba, to be exact. Leaves at 8 A.M. for the capital city of Languka."

Startled, Carstairs said, "*Africa* . . . what the hell was he doing *there*? And where on earth is Ubangiba? Have we any information on it?"

"Somewhere," said Bishop. "Actually I seem to remember it being in the newspapers recently but I can't recall why or when. Will the Department's abridged Africa notes do?"

"Anything," said Carstairs.

The file on Ubangiba, once on his desk, did not have much to say about the country. In the past two decades it had possessed two other names and seemed to be mostly known for its recurring coups. Otherwise it was just another small sub-Saharan country, half of its land fertile enough to grow crops, the rest sand, desert, and goat-herding nomads. Its exports were animal hides, sunflower seeds, and groundnuts. It had gained its independence in 1981; the first elected President had been assassinated; the second President had been ousted in a 1989 coup by a Daniel Simoko, who had proclaimed himself President-for-Life.

No industry, no oil, mused Carstairs. *No terrorist groups either.* Still, he couldn't help but wonder what had drawn Henry Bidwell to such a desolate country five times in the past four and a half months.

Unless Paris had been careless and there was another flight 1192 they'd missed.

With a sigh he returned to his paperwork, wished Bidwell a happy return from whatever nightmares he must be enduring in captivity, and promptly forgot about him.

CHAPTER 4

"SARDINES!" CRIED MRS. POLLIFAX SUDdenly as they headed north on I-95, still followed by the green sedan.

"I beg your pardon?" said Kadi. She was seated boldly in the front seat now, but keeping a low profile.

"Sardines," repeated Mrs. Pollifax. "I've been trying and *trying* to puzzle out why these people searched the house and found nothing, but still seem to think you were hiding there." She added grimly, "Four empty sardine tins in the storage closet, two empty cola cans, and no doubt bread crumbs as well. Idiotic of me to forget that, we never removed them."

"I forgot them, too," said Kadi sadly. "I can be quite intelligent when I'm not frightened but I never thought of them either. And I suspect you were quite distracted by finding me in your house. You really think they saw the empty tins and guessed?"

"In any thorough search they would definitely see them," said Mrs. Pollifax. "They're what I noticed in the closet even before I saw you and I can think of no other reason why they're still following us. Kadi, I think it's time you tell me what this is all about, and why I shouldn't take you to the nearest police station where you'd be safe."

"I'm not sure that I *would* be safe," said Kadi soberly. "And I don't really know what it's all about except that Sammy's in trouble. Real trouble, I think, but I can't prove it and nobody would believe me."

"Try me," said Mrs. Pollifax, giving her a quick glance. "Who is Sammy?"

She said cautiously, "A boy I grew up with. In another country, which is why nobody here would find it important. I forgot Yale is in New Haven, and anyway I hadn't heard from Sammy since he came to the United States nearly four years ago, but suddenly there he was, walking toward me on the street in New Haven, and his eyes lighted up and he raced toward me and we hugged. And he was glad to see me. *Glad*," she repeated.

"Of course," murmured Mrs. Pollifax.

"But then the young man with him joined us, and Sammy changed," Kadi said. "Sammy introduced him as his roommate, Clarence Mulimo, and suddenly he was very formal. I said why didn't we have a cup of coffee and talk, because we were standing right next to a coffee shop. His roommate shook his head and said something to Sammy that I didn't hear, but Sammy insisted. And that's when it all happened."

"What happened?"

Kadi was silent, remembering the shabby coffee shop, nearly empty, and how Sammy and his friend had sat across from her, and how she'd asked Sammy how his mother was.

"He said, 'She is very well, thank you, *and how are your parents, Kadi*?' "

She turned her face to Mrs. Pollifax and added quietly, "That really startled me, you see, because he knows very well that my parents are dead. He was trying to tell me something but I didn't know what, so I just asked how he liked college, and he asked me what had brought me to New Haven. A job interview, I said, but I didn't think I'd pleased them.

"And then his roommate said 'Excuse me' and headed for the men's room and I was so relieved, and I said 'Sammy'—"

She hesitated, her voice unsteady. "Right away Sammy placed a finger warningly to his lips, and then he reached under the table where Clarence had been sitting and brought out a tiny plastic object that had been attached there with a suction cup. Some kind of listening device."

"An electronic bug," said Mrs. Pollifax, extremely interested now.

Kadi nodded. "He put it back and then drew out a pencil and scrap of paper, and while I talked idiotically about the weather, and missing home, he wrote three words, and when he handed me the slip of paper it read NOT ROOMMATE—GUARD.

"I just gaped at him, I mean I was terribly alarmed and awfully puzzled, too, but I shoved the note in my pocket and asked what courses he was taking at Yale and then I told him, 'Your roommate's returning, Sammy, he seems very nice.'

"And then," she said shakily, "then Sammy reached inside his shirt and drew out—"

She stopped, and Mrs. Pollifax glanced at her. "Yes?" she prodded.

Steadying her voice Kadi said, "It was a ball of pink modeling clay, the kind you see in toy shops, the sort that children play with, or maybe an adult would use like worry beads. I didn't understand until he peeled away a tiny corner of it—to show me what it concealed. It was so valuable it made me gasp. And then his hand went under the table with it, I reached under the table, too, he placed it in my hand and I dropped it quickly in my pocket."

Mrs. Pollifax said lightly, "And what was it he gave you?"

She shook her head. "That's Sammy's secret, so I can't tell you, but I knew I couldn't stay any longer, I said I'd have to catch my bus now, and—and I went out, very worried, knowing something was wrong, and outside there was parked this white van with those crazy misspelled words Chigi Scap Metal. I began to walk the four blocks to the bus station but

I'd not gone far when I realized the van was slowly following me."

"Did they try to approach you?"

"No, because I started to run and I raced into the bus station, the New York bus was there and filling with passengers so I climbed on it right away. But one of the men must have left the van to see where I was going because when the bus started for New York the van was behind it."

"But you didn't go to New York," Mrs. Pollifax reminded her.

In the light of the dashboard Kadi looked miserable. "No, I panicked. I thought they wanted to find out where I live, and I knew they mustn't. The bus stopped in Bridgeport and I thought of leaving it there but I was too scared, so I didn't, but then later we began passing houses and gardens, and I thought of asking the bus driver to please stop—and he did—because I run very fast. I thought I could lose them easily on foot."

"Except you didn't."

"No, and they almost caught me, the two men. One of them chased me through back yards, and if you hadn't been in your garden—" Her voice broke. "Now they're still after me, Mrs. Pollifax, and what are we going to do?"

Mrs. Pollifax said calmly, "I don't know yet, but I have a full tank of gas, my car is very good on mileage, that green sedan looks quite old, a real 'gas guzzler,' and it's possible they may run out of gas before we do, and have to stop. I think we simply keep driving north and hope. But tell me, Kadi, in what country did you and Sammy grow up?"

"Most people have never heard of it," she explained soberly. "It's in Africa. My parents were missionary-doctors, you see. It's a small country. It's called Ubangiba now."

By half-past nine Mrs. Pollifax had grown tired of driving; Kadi had volunteered to help but she had no license, and in any case the green sedan remained resolutely behind them and Mrs. Pollifax did not care to risk the consequences if they stopped even for a moment. Noticing how tired Kadi looked by the light of the dashboard Mrs. Pollifax resisted making any more demands on her, and their conversation had become polite and desultory; she had learned how to say hello—*moni*—in the language of Ubangiba, and that Kadi was studying drawing and woodcarving at art school, but by now Mrs. Pollifax was definitely looking forward to a bed and some sleep after the day's rather disturbing encounters. She interrupted the silence to say firmly, "Obviously my theory about their running out of gas has been rapidly running out of possibility."

"Yes," Kadi said politely.

"And we need sleep."

"Oh yes," agreed Kadi.

Mrs. Pollifax nodded. "Somehow we've got to lose them, and it can't be done on a highway. A city is best, and I should have tried it miles ago." She pointed. "We're approaching Worcester, it could be risky. Are you game?"

Kadi said with spirit, "How can you ask? The word bed is right now the loveliest word I can think of, I haven't slept in one since Sunday."

Mrs. Pollifax gave her a quick glance and smiled. "Off we go then," she said, turning down the exit ramp. "I think we need a place for the night near the highway, in case a fast getaway becomes necessary. Nothing fancy, more like that," she said, pointing, as they passed a rundown motel with a bright neon sign proclaiming it the Bide-A-Wee. "We'll aim for that later."

Having found a goal she now applied herself to losing the green sedan by driving up one street and down another, always taking care to remain in the neighborhood of the Bide-A-Wee lest she not find it again. They spent twenty-five minutes racing traffic lights before they turned red, except the green sedan disdainfully ignored the red traffic lights anyway, and continued to tailgate them until abruptly a small miracle occurred. Kadi said exultantly, "They've stopped! They've stopped, Mrs. Pollifax! The light turned red for them but *this* time there's a police cruiser behind them waiting for the light to change, and they *had* to stop!"

Mrs. Pollifax sighed with relief. "Let's fervently hope we can find the Bide-A-Wee again, and quickly. I remember it having lots of parking space, too," she said, and several minutes later she was pulling into the parking lot beside the motel and maneuvering her car between two small pick-up trucks. "We'll ask for a room overlooking the car," she said firmly. "I shall insist."

Presently they were ensconced in room 211, and while Kadi showered in the bathroom Mrs. Pollifax turned on the small television to a flickering screen and to a voice saying, "It has now been six days since Henry Bidwell was abducted, and if the police have any clues as to his abductors they are keeping them private. . . . Bidwell's wife is under a doctor's care, and his employers are offering a reward of fifty thousand dollars to anyone with information as to his whereabouts. . . . In Paris today, OPEC met again and the price of oil . . ."

Mrs. Pollifax snapped it off and sat down on the bed, longing for a toothbrush. Kadi came out of the bathroom and said, "It's your turn," and lay down on the opposite bed and promptly fell asleep. Mrs. Pollifax lay down on her own bed and then, perversely, found herself wide awake and not sleepy at all.

I'm uneasy, she thought, frowning, *but I've been uneasy all' day, why can't I sleep now?* At last, long after ten o'clock, she left her bed to stand at the window and gaze out at the lights of the city, her glance eventually moving to the street below, and finally to her car, and then across the street to the bright lights of a larger motel. She watched as a car drove into the entrance of the motel across the street, disappeared and soon emerged at the other side—*circling it,* realized Mrs. Pollifax, suddenly alert—

and as the car drove toward the Bide-A-Wee it passed under a street light and it was a dark green sedan.

Chilled, Mrs. Pollifax realized that Kadi's pursuers were methodically checking every motel in the area for her red car.

There is something frighteningly important about this, she thought, *they're merciless, what will they ever do to Kadi if they overtake her, what do they want of her?*

"Kadi," she said in a low voice, "Kadi, wake up, they're about to find us."

The girl was on her feet at once. "Where?"

"We've got to leave," Mrs. Pollifax told her. "And *fast.*"

Kadi was beside her, shrugging into her tweed jacket. Mrs. Pollifax picked up the phone and called the desk clerk. "We need a taxi, please—quickly—it's an emergency."

"Emergency?" mumbled a sleepy voice.

"We need a hospital—*hurry*!"

The desk clerk, sufficiently aroused, said, "Cab—right, I'll call."

"How long?"

"Three to five minutes, I'd guess."

She fervently hoped he guessed right.

"What on earth," Kadi said, staring at her, open-mouthed.

"You're having an attack of appendicitis," Mrs. Pollifax told her crisply. "Fetch your knapsack, I'll carry it down. . . . Walk bent over and clutching your stomach."

"But why? What about your car?"

"Take a look out the window," Mrs. Pollifax told her. "They're going to find it in about two minutes. No, they've already found it, they're shining a flashlight on the license plate."

Kadi looked stricken. "Oh God."

Mrs. Pollifax opened the door. "Quickly—lean on me. Be *sick*, Kadi."

"I *feel* sick," gasped Kadi as they raced down the stairs.

CHAPTER 5

IT WAS HALF-PAST TEN AND CARSTAIRS was working late in his office, quite alone; Bishop was presumably asleep or out nightclubbing. Carstairs had just completed the last of his work when the next day's Departmental bulletin could be heard arriving on his fax machine. He yawned and thought of ignoring it until morning, but after a moment's reflection he tore it from the machine and glanced through it. There was the usual review of progress—he skipped this—and with more interest turned to the Departmental FYI memos, which so often held juicy gossip and rumors from around the world. NOT FOR PUBLIC CONSUMPTION, he read: FBI reports first attempt at delivering

Bidwell ransom failed, unidentifiable sources report 50 million demanded . . .

"Good old 'Unidentifiable Source,' " murmured Carstairs, but fifty million was a hell of a lot of money, in fact it had to set a record; *someone* found Bidwell of great value. His glance slid to Memo: MIDDLE EAST DEPT.: Iran. Two Europeans reported arriving Teheran private plane, met by top government limo, i.d.'d by "friendly parties" as Yule Romanovitch, A. Lecler.

Carstairs yawned again, put aside the bulletin and rose from his desk to go home when abruptly he sat down and picked up the Departmental bulletin again: the names Romanovitch and Lecler had struck him as vaguely familiar and he wondered why. Frowning, he leaned back in his chair and attempted an emptying of his mind, hoping the answer might spring from his subconscious as so frequently happened; in fact he sometimes found his subconscious more reliable than Bishop's memos as he juggled three and four projects at a time.

Got it! he remembered: *the FBI inquiry on the kidnapped Bidwell.* Springing from his chair he went to the files and there they were, the same names scrawled in the engagement book that Bidwell had kept locked in an office drawer, the same two men, surely, that Bidwell had met several times in Paris: Lecler and Romanovitch, like a vaudeville team.

He wondered if Mornajay was still Upstairs in his office, and rang his number. Mornajay had left, however in Europe it was almost morning: he put in a call to Bernard of the Interpol in Paris at his home and was presently connected.

"Bernard," he said, "I'd like to know what you might have, if anything, on a Yule Romanovitch and one Achille Lecler." Glancing over the list he added, "Also, a Rogere Desforges."

"Hmmmm," murmured Bernard, "give me half an hour, will you? But I can tell you at once who Rogere Desforges is. You will find him easily enough in your *Who's Who*, he is one of our geophysicists, very well known."

"Geophysicist," repeated Carstairs, frowning. "Right—get back to me, will you?"

"Burning the candle?" suggested Bernard. "Or whatever the idiom is?"

"That's right, Bernard, at both ends."

Forty minutes later Carstairs received Bernard's return call. "What we have on these two men," he said, "is limited and murky. The two are middlemen, involved in a number of questionable deals, and probably more that are unknown to us. Lecler has a New York office as well as an office in Paris. In New York he is Lecler Consultants, in Paris he is L-V Investment Company. They operate just inside the law, barely, so that we've never been able to pin anything on them but we'd love to."

"Interesting," said Carstairs. "Any known connection with terrorist groups?"

"I'd say absolutely out of character," replied Bernard. "They're very suave and subtle, these two, but strictly non-political. To my knowledge they've never been associated with violence of that sort. Dirty deals, yes, but that's another category."

Carstairs hesitated and then he said, "Would you hazard a guess as to why an American businessman would contact them separately, or together, a number of times on his visits to Paris?"

"My friend," said Bernard, "I do not like to be overly suspicious but I would take a close look at whatever company your American businessman represents, which is—?"

"A holding company," said Carstairs.

"Ah yes, my friend, but does one know what it 'holds'? Such a splendid word, 'holding,' and your American laws are a little loose, are they not? But please, I do not wish to be so negative, yet still—"

"I understand," Carstairs told him. "And thanks, Bernard."

"You'll share? As I said—"

"Definitely," Carstairs told him, "but for the moment it's mere curiosity and speculation." He hung up with a sigh. For all practical purposes he had reached a dead end, but still it remained odd, a man like Bidwell associating with two men of such dubious reputations that their dossiers were recorded at Interpol. He had learned little that interested him except for the fact that Rogere Desforges was a geophysicist.

Geophysicist, he repeated, and scowled. There was something there. Not graspable yet, but lurking.

He decided that it was time to learn more about this Ubangiba that had so interested Bidwell that he had made five trips there inside of four and a half months. He had told Bernard that his inquiry was mere curiosity and speculation but it was more than that: those blank pages in Bidwell's engagement calendar still bothered him; they did not fit a man whose life Addams had called an open book.

Switching off phones and computers, he extinguished the lights in both offices, and with his coat under his arm headed for the Reference Room. Here, surrounded by atlases, directories, phone books, and updated files on every country in the world, he placed his coat over a chair and began by looking up Claiborne-Osborne International. The words *syndicates* and *consortiums* were prominent, and he ran his eyes down the list: foreign banks, oil-drilling, hydro-electric power, earth-moving machinery . . . active in Tunisia, Algeria, Egypt, and Pakistan . . . offices in Cairo and Paris, main office in New York.

He reflected dryly that rather a lot of terrorist possibilities existed there, except that he had no idea why anyone would single out Henry Bidwell to kidnap. No link there.

But there was one country missing from that list of Claiborne-Osborne's interests, and that was Ubangiba.

Pulling out more books he came at last to an in-depth history of the country and began to read attentively. It seemed the area now called Ubangiba was first mentioned in 1783 by one Ebu Taylor, lone survivor of a Sahara caravan wiped out by the Tuareg. Rescued by a tribe called the Shambi, he was taken to "a pastoral land where the Shambi and Soto tribes lived in peace under the benign rule of a King Zammat."

"Local myth," he read, "has it that centuries earlier a quarrel arose between Chief Mombolu of the Soto tribe, and Zammat, chief of the Shambi tribe. To avoid war it was decided by the wisemen of the country that both men should be bound together in a room into which two poisonous snakes would be released, and in that manner the gods would decide which man would survive to be ruler of both tribes. It was Chief Mombolu who died, and Zammat whom the gods favored."

Carstairs thought dryly, *Interesting way to run an election.*

"From that time on," he read, "the King's totem has been a pair of intertwined serpents, represented on both the sacred royal gold ring that only the King can wear, and later by the flag of the country, on which two serpents repose on a scarlet background."

Carstairs skipped ahead to World War I, where Britain, rather against its will, inherited the country by the Treaty of Versailles.

"The British effort to dethrone the King," he read, "roused violent protests from the people. Ultimately, a Parliament was allowed under the King; a railroad was built but never used, an attempt made at a cement factory that went bankrupt, and the country fell into decay. The British maintained a consulate and gave minimal financial aid but basically the country was considered unrewarding. It continued as a Kingdom until King Zammat VIII, educated at Oxford, negotiated independence from the British and prepared his country for free election of a President.

"At his death," it concluded, "the sacred royal gold ring disappeared, and because of this the tribes have since regarded with distrust the ensuing rulers, including King Zammat's popular son, who was the first and only elected President, but who died mysteriously five months later. According to the belief of the people, he was poisoned by two serpents angered by the loss of the sacred royal ring, and they have regarded this as the reason for their many misfortunes since then."

And a good many misfortunes there had been, concluded Carstairs, noting the riots, droughts, and coups that followed. One more restless African country; obviously it was time to forget Ubangiba, yet he continued to stare at the map of the small elongated country, impoverished, threatened by drought, overlooked and forgotten, scarcely worth invasion by ambitious neighbors. What had been Claiborne-Osborne's interest in Ubangiba? Had Bidwell made enemies there?

He decided that in the morning he would arrange for someone to interview Claiborne-Osborne International and learn just what they planned to develop there. Until he knew what lay behind those concealed trips to the country, there had to remain the suspicion that Bidwell's abduction was somehow tied to Ubangiba.

He knew better now than to question his curiosity;

there was something about Bidwell's secret 1192 flights that troubled him, and he had no idea why.

Bishop, more knowledgeable, would have said it was what made him special, an almost psychic quality that led him to follow his instincts against all reason.

CHAPTER 6

DESCENDING AT TOP SPEED INTO THE tiny lobby of the Bide-A-Wee, Mrs. Pollifax flung bills and key at the desk clerk just as a cab drove up to the lighted entrance. "In you go," she told Kadi, and opening the taxi door, "Nearest hospital, please—in a hurry!"

The driver glanced at Kadi and said, "Right on, lady." As he headed out into the street Mrs. Pollifax glanced back and saw two shadowy men approach the lighted entrance. It was too dark to see their faces but she and Kadi had been seen entering the cab. She knew this because the two figures abruptly halted in surprise and, as the cab drove away, she saw them race back toward their own car . . . to follow.

Kadi said, "But Mrs. Pollifax, a *hospital*?"

"Trust me," she said.

The taxi drew up to the huge lighted entrance. "City Hospital, ma'am. Five bucks."

"Yes," she said, fumbling for bills. "Where are we, what corner is this, what streets?"

"Chandler and Park, ma'am."

They hurried up the steps to the admissions entrance and through the doors, where Mrs. Pollifax led Kadi to the long row of chairs along one wall and said firmly, "Sit."

"But where are you going?"

"To that public telephone over there."

She was quite familiar with the number by now. It might be nearly midnight, but in the Baltimore offices of William Carstairs, attorney-at-law, the lights would be on all night, and someone always at the switchboard.

A bright voice answered almost at once. "Legal office," it chirped.

"Is this Betsey?" asked Mrs. Pollifax.

"Yes it is, but who—*Mrs. Pollifax*?"

"Yes, and I'm in trouble, Betsey, I need help, is there someone—*someone*—to talk to?"

"I'll put you through at once," she said efficiently, and a moment later a sleepy voice said, "Bishop here," and yawned into the receiver.

"Bishop, it's me—Emily Pollifax—and I need help," she told him. "Badly. I can't explain why because I don't know, but my house has been searched and I've been chased across Connecticut and they're still following. Do you have any safe place for us to go—what you call a 'safe house' for hiding?"

At the Department people did not ask unnecessary questions. Bishop merely said, "Where are you at this precise moment, Mrs. P?"

"In Worcester, Massachusetts, at City Hospital, corner Chandler and Park, with a companion feigning appendicitis, but we came in a taxi and they may have followed us here, too."

Bishop said, "Give me the number you're calling from, I'll get back to you in five minutes. Can you hang on?"

"There are lights and people here," she told him, but her voice trembled a little from tiredness and the beginnings of a fear that she couldn't name.

"Five minutes," Bishop told her reassuringly.

She hung up and looked around her. Finding Kadi, she smiled as cheerfully as she could but refused to relinquish her position by the telephone to join her. She thought it the longest five minutes that she had lived through in a long time, and when the phone rang she interrupted its first ring.

"Bishop here," he said.

"Yes."

"Stay where you are, near people. Inside of thirty minutes a young man named Pete will meet you there, he has your description, and *he'll* be wearing a black leather jacket and red sweater. We've found a 'safe house' for you—a rather odd one but safe."

"Bless you, Bishop," said Mrs. Pollifax, and marveled at his asking no questions because she had absolutely no idea what she could have said in reply.

"But who did you call?" asked Kadi wonderingly as she joined her.

"A friend," said Mrs. Pollifax. "There'll be a man coming for us in half an hour, wearing a black leather jacket and red sweater, and Kadi, I want to know—I *must* know about your friend Sammy now. Can you believe him, can you trust him, and all that he implied? That he's in *danger*?"

Kadi gave her a startled glance. "*Yes*, I believe him, and *yes*, I trust him, and if you doubt me I can tell you what my father said of him, and my father taught him at the missionary school, and loved him like a son. He said, 'Young Sammy will be a *good* leader of his people, there's no cruelty in him, and he is bright, very bright.' But his eyes were no longer bright when I met him," she said sadly.

"Leader? What do you mean leader?" asked Mrs. Pollifax.

"Well," explained Kadi earnestly, "Ubangiba used to be a kingdom, it was one of the last countries to gain its independence, which is when the King decreed that it would be a democracy, and he set the date for elections. But then he died, you see, he was very old but—" She frowned. "But also very wise, I think. His son was very popular and he was expected to be elected President, and he was, but five months later he died quite mysteriously—they think poisoned."

"Oh dear," said Mrs. Pollifax. "And then?"

"Then no more elections," Kadi said sadly. "Mr. Chinyata took over and made himself President-for-Life and nearly ruined what was left of the country. There were food riots, people were hungry, and after that there was another coup—which," said Kadi, her voice trembling a little, "was when my parents were shot. It was General Simoko who next made himself President-for-Life, except really he is a dictator."

"Your parents shot!" exclaimed Mrs. Pollifax, startled. "My dear, I'm terribly sorry to hear that—but Kadi, I have to ask you what connection this has with your friend Sammy."

Kadi sighed. "Well, you see, Sammy's grandfather was King Zammat VIII, back when there was a King, and it was Sammy's father who became the first and only elected President and then died. And Sammy dropped the *Z* to be *Sammat*."

Mrs. Pollifax sat very still, absorbing this startling fact so casually tossed at her. *Not Sammy but Sammat,* she thought, and felt glimmerings of understanding. She did not know what she understood yet—it all sounded very exotic and foreign to her—but vague possibilities occurred to her, unclear as yet, and convoluted, but spelling wickedness. "So he is not just Sammy," she murmured, "but Sammat, grandson of a King and son of a President. Who sent him to Yale, Kadi, do you know?"

"I don't know," Kadi said miserably. "But he is there, with a roommate who isn't a roommate."

Mrs. Pollifax nodded. "And who presumably has you followed," she added soberly. "It's a pity we couldn't have stopped in New Haven and kidnapped Sammy."

"Could we go back?" Kadi asked eagerly. "Could we rescue him?"

Mrs. Pollifax shook her head. "You've become dangerous to them, Kadi, presumably because you're a friend of Sammy's. Besides, it's too late," she told her, seeing a tanned young man in a black leather jacket and red sweater approach them. "We can only find safety for *you* just now."

Planting himself in front of her the young man said, "I'm Pete, any luggage?"

Mrs. Pollifax shook her head. "No luggage."

He glanced curiously at Kadi. "Car's just outside, slide fast into the back seat."

There was a driver already at the wheel, making their getaway very fast, the car in motion the moment the doors slammed. But looking back Kadi said, "They're there, Mrs. Pollifax, they must have found out from the cab driver where he took us."

"Being followed, are we?" said Pete, glancing back.

"Green sedan."

He nodded. "Okay . . . this is Tom, driving, we'll try to lose them but it doesn't matter now if we don't."

"Doesn't matter?" echoed Mrs. Pollifax. "Where are we going?"

"A small private airport. Orders are to tuck you away safe—you must have clout, lady."

Kadi gave her a quick, puzzled glance but said nothing.

They had left the city behind them when the car turned down a narrow road, its headlights picking out a field and several small planes grouped around a hangar. They were deposited next to a helicopter with its motor already idling. Mrs. Pollifax and Kadi were ushered out by Pete, the car turned and sped away.

"In you go," said Pete, boosting them up into the helicopter.

"You too?"

"I'm the pilot," he told her with a grin, and latching the door behind them he took his place at the controls. The rotoblades began to turn faster and faster, and suddenly they were being lifted from the earth into the night sky.

"Mrs. Pollifax," said Kadi in a small voice, "am I being kidnapped?"

Mrs. Pollifax glanced at her tired anxious face and said calmly, "I think we both are. I admit that I didn't expect this, either, but I trust my friend and you must, too. Difficult as it may be at this moment," she added dryly.

Kadi said wonderingly, "Your friend must be very powerful, Mrs. Pollifax."

"Well, you see," Mrs. Pollifax told her with a smile, "I send him a fruitcake every Christmas."

Kadi laughed shakily.

The earth lay below them like a patchwork quilt of flickering lights followed by great dark spaces of land. Presently Kadi fell asleep, which Mrs. Pollifax thought a great blessing; she would have preferred to sleep, too, but it was night, which she had always found the least secure season of the day for confronting Unknowns, and she was too tired to sleep. She had to remind herself that she really could never, *never* have abandoned this girl to the thugs pursuing her, and that wherever they were going it had been arranged by Bishop, but it was necessary to hold firmly to this because it was taking a very long time to reach whatever safe place he'd found for them.

Too long a time, she thought, after a glance at her watch told her that it was past one o'clock in the morning of a new day, and that they were into their second hour of flight.

Responsibility, she sighed, naming it. . . . *I have made myself responsible for this Kadi who spent two days and nights huddled in our closet out of fear.*

Obviously she was not going to be present at the afternoon's Garden Club meeting.

She began to think of Kadi's Ubangiba and what it might be like. Africa was such a huge continent and she had seen only one African country, and that had been on the Zambezi River. She supposed there were similarities nevertheless: the attractive capital with its villas and its roads laid out by early colonialists, and beyond this elegance the shanty towns, and then the countryside where women, erect, barefooted, and proud, walked along the roadside carrying huge baskets on their heads filled with kindling or food, and there were glimpses through the trees of dirt paths leading to thatch-roofed villages. She wondered if Kadi's Ubangiba had baobab trees silver in the sunlight, and towering anthills as high as a man's waist.

She realized the helicopter was flying lower now and beginning its descent. Peering out of the window she saw a blaze of light ahead in the dark countryside and wondered what it could possibly be: *surely not another airport,* she thought with a sinking heart. She nudged Kadi and said, "We're landing, Kadi."

The helicopter banked and turned and she lost sight of the cloud of brightness until it reappeared in the window across the aisle, but at a distance; the helicopter was coming down now, making its uncanny horizontal drop to the earth. They landed with a slight jarring in the middle of a dark field.

"Where are we?" asked Kadi, rubbing her eyes.

"We're here," Pete told her. "Don't worry, you're expected." He crawled past them, unlatched the door, and jumped down to help them out.

With the opening of the hatch a flood of noise rushed at them: muted shouts and screams, and underlying these the sounds of rollicking music, while—emerging out of that distant brilliance—Mrs. Pollifax saw a man with a flashlight making his way toward them across the dark field.

She said in consternation, "But where are we?"

"Rural Maine," said Pete. "You'll have to move back, I'm taking off again now."

Bewildered, Mrs. Pollifax said, "But have you brought us to the right place? This surely can't be a safe house."

"Nothing beats it," Pete said.

"But that's merry-go-round music—it's a carnival!" shouted Mrs. Pollifax.

"You got it," grinned Pete, and with a flip of his hand he closed the hatch and, a moment later, at the controls again, he set the rotoblades turning. The helicopter rose in a gust of cold wind, leaving them standing in the middle of the dark field waiting for the man with the flashlight.

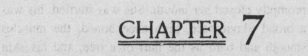

CHAPTER 7

A LIGHT WAS TURNED ON EACH OF THEIR faces, and behind its blinding flash Mrs. Pollifax could see the shape of a burly man and the outline of a limp, wide-brimmed hat.

"Name's Willie," he said without preamble. "Watch your step, follow me."

He guided them across untilled earth toward the blaze of lights. Ahead of them, rising out of its brilliance like a great spider web, Mrs. Pollifax saw a towering ferris wheel that slowed and then stopped, its pause eliciting a fresh burst of screams from those at the top, but even these couldn't blot out the undercurrent of noise from below that sounded to Mrs. Pollifax like a buzzing swarm of angry bees in a hive. She could see nothing more of the carnival than the ferris wheel because a cluster of trailers intervened, and it was toward one of these that Willie led them. Emerging into the dimly lighted circle of trailers they paused and she saw Willie's face for the first time, and Mrs. Pollifax, in the act of yawning, promptly closed her mouth. She was startled: his was a broad Slavic face, high cheekboned, the muscles smooth and hard as the burl of a tree, and his skin dark as a gypsy's. Not a man to cross in an argument, she was thinking, and in no way did he resemble a manager in his faded jeans and shirt, yet the sign on the door of the trailer read MANAGER. He opened it and stood back for them to enter.

They walked into a warm, over-furnished living room where Mrs. Pollifax counted two couches and a startling number of lamps and overstuffed chairs; on one wall hung a gaudy poster advertising Willie's Traveling Amusement Shows, and next to it a picture of Elvis Presley painted on black velvet. With a nod to a dazed-looking Kadi he said, "Your daughter can wait here, I'll ask you kindly to step into my office, I've a few words to say." He spoke with a faint accent that Mrs. Pollifax couldn't identify but struck her as familiar, if she could only think where she'd heard it before.

"Not my daughter," explained Mrs. Pollifax. "Her name is Kadi, spelled K-a-d-i."

He gave her a sharp glance. "African name, isn't it?"

"Yes," said Kadi, surprised.

Mrs. Pollifax was surprised, too, and looked at him with sudden respect.

He led her into an office where he pulled out a chair for her at one side of the large desk while he seated himself behind it and returned her frank stare with ironic interest. With a glance at the clock on the wall, he said, "I won't keep you long, it's nearly two o'clock, the carnival closes at two."

She said incredulously, "But—a *carnival*? Run by the Department?"

He looked pained. "Never say that, *ever*. When bankruptcy threatens it's Willie's Rich Uncle who rescues. No Department, no names. Willie's Rich Uncle. *Remember* that."

"Yes," she said meekly, and stifled another yawn. "But it's certainly inventive."

Studying her face he frowned. "They tell me you're experienced." He said bluntly, "You don't look experienced. They want you to help."

She said politely, "That was very kind of Bish—of Willie's Rich Uncle," and then, sharply, "What do you mean '*help*'?"

"We've had an accident here," he said. "A few minutes after midnight, too late to stop you coming, you were already on the way. I had to make a call to Baltimore—"

Poor Bishop, thought Mrs. Pollifax, twice interrupted in his sleep.

"—because of the accident."

"Accident," she repeated, stifling another yawn.

"A very suspicious one. It's been suggested you help while you're here."

Mrs. Pollifax was not so sleepy that she didn't understand the inference. She said quickly, "Oh, but I can't stay, it's Kadi who was in danger, we only met this morning—no, yesterday morning, and thanks to Bishop—"

"Willie's Rich Uncle," he pointed out.

"No, *BISHOP*," she said flatly, in revolt now. "Thanks to Bishop we were lifted completely out of a dangerous situation but I didn't expect *this*. My only interest is in seeing Kadi safe. I mean—" She stopped and fumbled for words, realizing that she'd not given a thought to anything but getting away from the Chigi Scap Metal people, and what *had* she expected? "I assumed I'd go home tomorrow," she told him. "Even Kadi could go back to her New York art school now. At least," she added doubtfully, "they couldn't trace her there. I don't *think*."

"You don't think," he mocked.

"I'm tired," she admitted, "it's been a long day. I must get in touch with—all right, Willie's Rich Uncle tomorrow about some help for Kadi. You do have a phone?"

"A temporary link-up, yes," he told her. "Of course—we're a business."

"You were saying there was an *accident*?"

He nodded. His skin had a luster to it in the light of the desk lamp like highly polished wood, and there was a gap between his two front teeth when he spoke. These details she noted from habit, just as he too, she knew, was taking pains to read her face and learn who and what she was. "Yes," he said. "To Lazlo, sent here for protection—like you and the girl."

"That's a calculated hit," she told him.

He suddenly smiled, and she realized that she might eventually like him.

He leaned forward across the desk to emphasize his words. "So I'll tell you. . . . Sometime after midnight there was a shout of 'Hey Rube,' which—" he explained, seeing her look blank, "is the signal in any carnival for trouble. Like everybody else Lazlo picked up a tent stake and joined the others down by the gate. And that," he said heavily, "is where somebody in the crowd stuck a knife in his back."

"Stuck a—was he killed? Is he alive?"

"Barely. He's in the hospital, in critical condition—and he was sent by Willie's Rich Uncle, you understand?"

She understood; strange as it might seem to find such a person in this bizarre environment he meant that Lazlo was an intelligence agent who had withstood dangers she could only imagine, and he had been sent here to be safe. And tonight someone had tried to kill him.

She said, frowning, "But you called it an accident!"

He leaned back in his chair, eyes narrowed. "I'm keeping this short because you'll see I've work to do, but what's important—and suspicious—is that after the ambulance took Lazlo away I couldn't find anyone who had shouted 'Hey Rube,' and not a single carnie reported having had any trouble to need one."

Startled by this she said, "But would they tell you?"

He glanced at his watch. "Most I can vouch for, they're back every season and they'd tell me, yes. I run a clean carnival, no fly-by-nighter gets in unless he can prove he's not parking his car behind his tent for a quick getaway after robbing the tip blind. A couple of the acts in the Ten-in-One are new—had to be, I have to take what I can get—and a couple of concessions are new to me. Those I can't vouch for."

"Perhaps there'd been a quarrel?" she hazarded.

His gaze was scornful. "Why should there be a quarrel? A good man, very quiet. Once he'd rested I put him to work collecting tickets for the merry-go-round. He bunked alone, I never saw him talk to anyone."

Mrs. Pollifax fought back another yawn, longing for sleep, and with the feeling that she'd already sustained enough shocks during the past hours, she struggled to make sense of everything he had told her. She said, "What sort of trouble usually produces this 'Hey Rube' you spoke of?"

He shrugged. "A townie who feels he's been cheated, a drunk trying to pick a fight. The whiz mob causing trouble—pickpockets that would be. One of the grifters playing too strong and taking a mark for everything he's got. Doesn't happen often."

"So you actually think," began Mrs. Pollifax, but he stopped her by rising from his chair.

"What I think I've got no proof of," he said flatly. "If it was someone from outside who traced him here they could be gone by now, *but how did they find him*? If there's a leak at Willie's Rich Uncle, that's something else. But if there's a rotten apple in my show, if somebody got planted here—" His eyes glittered. "*Somebody* knew enough about us to shout 'Hey Rube.' I can't be everywhere at once and they've told me you have good eyes and good instincts."

As she stood up, too, he said roughly, "You can surely spare a few days in spite of the danger?"

"Danger?" she repeated.

"Of course—to you and the girl. If Lazlo's cover got blown, somebody may know too much about a certain connection with Willie's Rich Uncle and blow this cover, too. The 'copter may have been heard landing, and God knows you don't look like a carnie, you'll stand out like a dog in a duck pond."

"Yes," she said, and realized that her jaws had begun to ache from yawning.

He looked her over critically. "But Willie's Uncle says you'll do. I'll see Gertie gets you some old clothes to wear. Any good at fortune telling?"

Startled, Mrs. Pollifax said, "I've never done any."

He nodded. "We'll think of something. The girl's small, the Professor's magic show can use a small girl to saw in half." With his hand on the door he paused. "That's for tomorrow, now I'll show you where to sleep, but what's your name?"

"Mrs. Pollifax, Emily Pollifax."

He shook his head. "Not here. Better be called Emmy something. Emmy Smith? Jones?"

Since she was married to Cyrus Reed she said dryly, "Reed?"

"Okay, Emmy Reed." He opened the door to the living room where Kadi sat patiently waiting. She jumped up at the sight of Mrs. Pollifax and said, "Is everything all right?"

She nodded. "Everything's all right, Kadi, we'll stay here for just a few days, if you agree. Just to be sure."

With a shiver Kadi said, "Oh, I'd like to be sure, yes."

Outside, the buzz of sounds from the midway had diminished, the ferris wheel had stilled, and the merry-go-round was silent. Willie led them past two brightly lighted trailers to a small and shabby dark one, and taking a key from his pocket he unlocked the door and pushed it open. "You'll have a quiet sleep, nobody wakes up here before ten or eleven," he told them. "We're here one more night and then Friday it's tear-down and we move on to the next town. Give you time to get acquainted." He walked around Kadi, reached inside and turned on a light that shone garishly on shabby walls and broken venetian blinds.

"Beds," said Kadi, pointing, as Willie left.

Mrs. Pollifax saw them: a pair of narrow bunk beds, each with a blanket folded at one end and a pillow lying at the other. She thought, *Well, if I've exchanged a frying pan for a fire, at least I'll face it rested tomorrow.* She stepped inside, sat down on the bed to test it, abruptly stretched out, turned over, and immediately fell asleep.

Kadi, surprised, looked down at her, and then with a smile she covered her with a blanket and gave Mrs. Pollifax a shy kiss on the cheek.

"*Zikomo,* friend," she whispered.

CHAPTER 8

WHEN CARSTAIRS ARRIVED IN HIS OFFICE the next morning he found Bishop at his desk drinking what was apparently his fourth cup of coffee, given the empties lined up beside the IN and OUT baskets. "Late night?" said Carstairs tactfully.

"Not the kind you think," Bishop told him gloomily. "I was called twice by Betsey during the night. In my bed, sound asleep. Now I'm trying to wake up. The first call was Mrs. Pollifax, who I sent to Willie's—"

"Mrs. Pollifax!" exclaimed Carstairs. "To Willie's? What happened? What on earth—"

"The second call," went on Bishop, interrupting him, "was from Willie himself, reporting an attempt made on one of our men there sometime around midnight. He's in the hospital, stabbed in the back and in critical condition."

Carstairs whistled through his teeth. "I don't like the sound of *that*. Who was it?"

"Lazlo, a.k.a. Aziz Kalad."

Carstairs looked stunned. "We smuggled him out of Iran four months ago, what the devil is he doing in hiding at Willie's?"

"We turned him over to Farnesworth, remember?" said Bishop. "Lazlo refused a leave, said after four years of undercover work in Iran he was too edgy to lie in the Caribbean sun or take any sort of vacation, said it would drive him crazy. He asked for quieter work to get back the taste of being free again. Farnesworth put him to work in Boston. Simple surveillance jobs, I believe."

Carstairs said angrily, "Couldn't have been very simple if he's ended up in a safe house. Damn it, he's invaluable to us. What does Willie think, a random knifing or did 'they' find him? In which case—"

"Willie finds it pretty suspicious," Bishop said. "It seems a call of 'Hey Rube' went out around midnight that sent everyone running to the gate, which is where Aziz—Lazlo, that is—was stabbed in the crowd, except that later Willie couldn't find anyone who had shouted this 'Hey Rube,' and what's more couldn't find anyone in the entire show who'd run into any trouble that demanded it."

"Damn," said Carstairs. "Willie's always been

snug harbor, a perfect back-up place. Does Farnesworth know about this?"

Bishop shook his head. "Not yet, I figured Willie's strictly our business."

"And so is Lazlo. Bishop, contact Farnesworth's office and tell them we need to know—top priority—why and how Lazlo happened to be at Willie's—to be knifed like a sitting duck. Details, Bishop, I want details."

As he rose from his desk Carstairs added with a frown, "And Mrs. Pollifax, what the devil's happened to her? She's not on assignment."

"There wasn't time to ask," Bishop told him. "Her call came through at eleven, before Willie's call. She sounded at the end of her tether, said she'd been chased from Connecticut to Massachusetts and was calling from Worcester's City Hospital where she'd taken refuge for the moment. She was asking for help."

"Alone?"

Bishop frowned. "I don't think so. . . . No, she mentioned a companion feigning appendicitis, that's how she put it. Not Cyrus, or she'd have said so."

Carstairs sighed. "Well, give her a call and find out. If it's fallout from one of her past assignments, and someone is tracking *her* down, too—"

Bishop shook his head. "Show people sleep until noon. A thought that turns me green with envy," he added. "Willie said she needed sleep pretty badly."

"Well, contact her later when you've time,"

growled Carstairs. "You've notified Upstairs about Lazlo?"

Bishop nodded. "They're setting things in motion, there's a guard posted now at the hospital in Ellsworth, Lazlo's in intensive care but they're checking everyone with access to the hospital."

"Good. Now, I've got a job for you," Carstairs told him. "If you can stay awake to do it. I want you to fly to New York—Helga can take over your desk for you—because I've set up an eleven A.M. appointment for you with the acting CEO at Claiborne-Osborne International." He dropped a file on Bishop's desk. "Reading material for you en route so you can ask intelligent questions."

Surprised, Bishop said, "Has the FBI cleared this visit, or are we being *sub rosa*?"

Carstairs said silkily, "When did the FBI ask us to check our files? We set our clocks back a day, Bishop, it's today they approached us. Or late yesterday. We're only following up their queries in regard to Bidwell versus terrorist groups in Europe."

Bishop gave him a long hard look. "All of which is camouflage for what specific question?"

Carstairs smiled at him benevolently. "Why, to learn what their interest is in Ubangiba, of course. Without revealing *our* interest."

"You mean *your* interest," Bishop told him accusingly. "I don't get it, I really don't. What is it you suspect?"

Carstairs's face sobered. "I honestly don't know, Bishop, but those blank pages in Bidwell's engagement book bother me, I can't get them out of my head . . . a book locked away in his drawer and therefore not for public consumption, or so one presumes, it troubles me, yes. And the man's been kidnapped, is being held for some incredible ransom, and why Bidwell, of all people?"

"He was featured in *Fortune* magazine last year," pointed out Bishop. "It was made clear enough then how rich he is. A billionaire, if I remember correctly. Enough to entice any nefarious schemer."

"Then why didn't they abduct him last year? Nobody's found any secrets in his life, yet he wrote no names on those blank pages, no record of appointments, left no clues—and now he's been kidnapped. I'm hoping your trip to New York will explain everything so that I can put it out of my head once and for all." He glanced at his wrist watch. "You'll miss your plane. Ah—here's Helga," he murmured as Bishop's secretary appeared in the doorway. "Get moving," he told his assistant. "Be subtle, be tactful. Take over, Helga—all hell's been breaking loose today."

"So I've heard," she said demurely, and seated herself at Bishop's desk and began gathering up the empty coffee cups.

Carstairs moved on to his office, where Departmental reports and data had begun collecting on his desk. The hospital to which Lazlo had been rushed in Ellsworth, Maine, reported him out of intensive care but not in stable enough condition yet to be flown to Boston to a specialist; the guards posted in the building reported no attempts to infiltrate, and no suspicious approaches. It was still possible, thought Carstairs, that Lazlo had simply been the victim of a random incident, some young local punk on drugs or out to prove his manhood. . . . With some relief he turned to the paperwork that was always waiting for him, and called in Helga to dictate further memos and reports.

He had finished lunch at his desk when Bishop phoned him from New York.

"Well?" growled Carstairs. "Has Claiborne-Osborne found plutonium in Ubangiba? A rich lode of gold, or possibly oil?"

Bishop did not immediately reply, and Carstairs stiffened. "Well?" he said sharply.

"Claiborne-Osborne International," Bishop said at last, "has never heard of Ubangiba. I had to show the acting CEO where the blasted place was on the map."

Carstairs said quickly, "Do you believe him?"

"He'd have to be a candidate for an Academy Award if he was lying," said Bishop. "He seemed honestly and genuinely puzzled by my query. When I pressed him, he called in a few other people who seemed just as blank on the subject."

"And?"

"I stopped on my way out to query Bidwell's secretary. She too had never heard Bidwell or anyone in the company refer to Ubangiba, but at least she reads the newspapers and knew the country existed."

"I see," murmured Carstairs. "Curiouser and curiouser . . . Good work, Bishop, I'd like to tell you to stay and sample a few fleshpots in the Big City but you're needed. Come home."

"Yes, sir. Incidentally, I'm calling from a bar where the TV news is turned on, and Bidwell's wife was just making a plea to her husband's kidnappers to release him."

"What's she like?" Carstairs asked idly.

"Very groomed, very top-drawer. Finishing school accent. I'd say nothing in her life's prepared her for this sort of thing."

"How's she taking it?"

"I detect a mix of shock and embarrassment, the embarrassment at having to be seen on television making such a public plea, and the shock as expected."

"Right. See you." After wishing him a good flight back Carstairs sat for some moments thinking about what Bishop had told him. If Bishop was right, then Bidwell's flights on 1192 had been strictly his own business, but what had taken him there so mysteriously?

One of Bidwell's appointments in Paris had been with a Rogere Desforges whom Bernard had identified as a geophysicist. Perhaps there was something graspable there: it was possible that Desforges had been more than a casual luncheon guest, but certainly it was time to find out.

Switching on his intercom he said, "Helga, bring me a *Who's Who*, will you? American, British, and French."

It would have taken Bishop three minutes to secure these; Carstairs could not help but notice that Helga needed twelve minutes to find them.

"Stand by," he told her, opening each one to D. "I'm looking up one Rogere Desforges, geophysicist, and if I've any luck you can put a call through to France for me and see if he's out geophysicing or reachable. I'd like to speak to him today. What time is it in Paris?"

"Seven o'clock in the evening, sir," Helga said crisply.

"Damn," swore Carstairs. "I see that his office is in Paris, his residence in Rouen. Try both, and keep your fingers crossed."

CHAPTER 9

KADI, WAKING IN THE MORNING, WAS NOT particularly startled at finding herself in a strange bed. She had slept under a number of roofs when she was being smuggled out of Ubangiba, after the coup that had cost her parents their lives, and from there she had gone to Ohio to live with an aunt and then to New York City to art school. She liked to think this was what Emerson called "revolutions" in a life that accustomed one to change. Her father had been very partial to Emerson.

There was a stirring in the bed across the narrow aisle, and seeing Mrs. Pollifax, Kadi abruptly remembered the last few days, and the fear that she'd lived with, and she felt a wave of gratitude toward this woman. This was followed by a frown because she found it very mysterious, Mrs. Pollifax summoning a pilot, a helicopter, and an escape from Chigi Scap Metal with such dispatch, rather like a genie producing a miracle.

She thought, *There is more to this than she's told me, and she is certainly not the person I first thought; there are dimensions here that interest me very much.*

But what a relief it was to feel safe!

She sat up as the door opened and a woman in jeans and a baseball cap walked in. "Hello, dearies," she said cheerfully, "I've some clothes for you, Willie's orders."

Mrs. Pollifax, waking, gave the woman a puzzled glance, saw Kadi, looked around the trailer and sat up, too. "Obviously I wasn't dreaming—I'm still here," she announced. "Hello, Kadi . . . And you?"

"I'm Gertie, Pogo's wife." She had a weathered midlife face under the baseball cap, and now she began to sort the clothes that she carried over one arm. "For you—jeans, socks, and T-shirt," she told Kadi, blithely tossing them at her. "And for the lady—Emmy Reed, isn't it? Nothing yet, but we're looking for a shirt and if you're cold tonight here's a sweater. A bit moth-eaten, but what the heck it's warm."

"Thank you very much," said Mrs. Pollifax, accepting her largesse. "And is there food in that little refrigerator?"

"Bless you no . . . Turn left when you leave and head out into the midway, breakfast's at the grab-joint. Cook-house," she explained. "Can't miss it, sign says BIGGEST HOTDOGS IN USA, and only place open." To Kadi she said, "You'll find the Professor there, you'll have to learn the ropes by six o'clock."

"For what?" asked Kadi.

"Why, to be sawed in half," she said in surprise, and went out, closing the door behind her.

Kadi looked at Mrs. Pollifax in astonishment. "I'm to be sawed in half and she called you Emmy Reed?"

"I'll explain later," Mrs. Pollifax told her, "but just now we need breakfast. And," she added with a smile, "after I've seen you sawed in half I must speak with Willie about certain matters, having been *quite* blurred last night. Let's go!"

"But—*sawed in half*?"

Mrs. Pollifax nodded. "It seems we must both sing for our supper while we're here, and join the carnival."

"Oh," said Kadi, brightening, "what *fun*!"

Mrs. Pollifax wasn't at all certain that it was going to prove fun, not if there was a murderer hiding among these people, but she could admire Kadi's attitude. They walked out onto the midway, past the transformer and the Loop-o-Plane and found the Professor waiting for them outside the tent that housed the portable kitchen. He strode toward them at once, happily measuring Kadi's smallness.

"She'll do, she'll do," he said triumphantly, and to Kadi, with a bow, "I'm the Professor, purveyor of magic and wizardry, enchantments and all the wonders of illusion. And you?"

"Kadi Hopkirk," she said eagerly.

Mrs. Pollifax, obviously of no importance to him in his world of wonders, looked at him with amusement. His most distinguishing feature was a bright yellow goatee trimmed to a knife-edged point; otherwise he was a rather pale and plainfaced middle-aged man with a dyed goatee and what looked to be a toupee dyed to match it. There was, however, an earring in his left ear, and his fingers glittered with rings and she found this satisfying: he was clearly a man who did the best with what he'd been given. He led them under the canvas to the counter and introduced them to Mickey. "Coffee and breakfast for them, Mick," he said. "On the double, we've work to do."

A few other carnies sat on stools, staring into space, not quite awake yet and not speaking. It was early for them, explained the Professor, and he bade them hurry through their eggs and fried potatoes so Kadi could be rehearsed. "Tatiana," he called to a glorious redhead, "this is the new girl. Come!"

The shapely redhead yawned, muttered words under her breath, and abandoned her coffee to follow them as the Professor led them out of the cookhouse, past the ferris wheel, and down the midway. "By daylight," he said, "it's a bleak and empty piece of earth but just wait 'til six P.M., this place will light up like the 4th of July . . . crowds, music, lights, glamour . . . !"

It did look bleak in the pale sunshine, conceded Mrs. Pollifax, its concession booths shuttered by canvas shades, the sawdust still damp underfoot with dew, and not a soul in sight. The Professor strode ahead of them toward the largest tent on the midway and stopped for them to admire it.

"This here's the Ten-in-One," he said. "Ten sideshows under one canvas, except we got only eight this month. And the platform's called the bally platform and I'll bet you never saw grander pictures anywhere."

"No indeed," admitted Mrs. Pollifax, almost assaulted by the gaudy canvases that hung over the platform: THE SNAKE WOMAN OF BORNEO depicted a dark and wild-haired woman wearing snakes on her lap and around her neck; EL FLAMO, FEARLESS FIRE-EATER, had faded somewhat in color but he stood regally in profile, very erect, with flames curling out of his mouth; JASNA THE KNIFE-THROWER ("one miss and he dies") stood poised in tights, knife in hand, while the man at whom she threw them was already framed by knives. The pictures marched side by side in a long line and for just a moment Mrs. Pollifax felt that stir of excitement she'd known as a child when she'd visited a carnival, and looking at Kadi, seeing her eyes wide with wonder, she smiled.

The Professor led them past the ticket booth and inside. "You believe in magic?" he asked Kadi.

"Of course I believe in magic," she said earnestly, "but it's impossible to saw a lady in half."

"Why?" asked the Professor, regarding her with amusement.

"Because you would no longer have a lady to saw in half for the next performance."

"Alas, she has the logical mind, but such an innocent! Have you visited a carnival before, young lady?"

Kadi shook her head. "I grew up in a country without them."

"What a sad country, I cry for it," he said dismissingly. "Now we practice. Precision is everything! Practice, practice!"

The space inside the big tent held a line of closed booths, but the main focal point was a stage at one end with several rows of bleachers facing it. The Professor switched on lights and from behind the stage's backdrop he pushed out a platform on wheels. "Who is Kadi replacing?" Mrs. Pollifax called to him.

"Shirley," he said. "She eats too much. Too big, very uncomfortable for her."

"Then why do you need Tatiana?" she asked.

"Ah, the disillusionment," he rued. "Sit—you will be the audience, we will perform for you. Kadi, Tatiana, come. As you see," he announced to Mrs. Pollifax from the stage, "we have two boxes resting on this platform, I slide them apart—they move, you see?" He slid them together. "Note also there are no trapdoors below, no mirrors. Now, Kadi, you will please climb into this box on the top and slide down into the platform under the boxes. See? In you go."

"That platform's too narrow," protested Kadi.

"You will go there, it is *not* too narrow. It only *looks* too narrow to contain a person, it was *designed* to look too narrow—all magic is illusion here! Climb in, please, when the act begins you will already be hidden inside."

Looking doubtful Kadi climbed into the gaudy box on top of the platform and apparently found a space in which to insert herself because she vanished from sight.

"Now we begin." He and Tatiana bowed and dramatically unhinged the fronts of each box, dropping them to prove they were empty and without mirrors. With fluttering gestures Tatiana was helped up and into the boxes atop the base where she lay down, after which the Professor closed the hinged sides, leaving only her head and feet extended at each end.

"Now, Kadi," he called, "you can hear me?"

There came a muffled reply.

"I will commence. I have closed the hinged sides—dramatically, of course—so only Tatiana's head and feet can now be seen. Pay attention, young Kadi, you are hearing me? Good. Now I will turn the platform around—in a big circle—you feel this?—to show the audience no tricks, no trapdoors, there is only Tatiana, and it is now, as I turn you on the wheels, and while Tatiana's feet are out of view of the audience, this is the signal for you to slide your feet up through the opening in the base and push them out, you understand? At the same moment, as the apparatus turns, Tatiana withdraws her feet, hugging her knees tight in her box, and you become Tatiana's feet, except—*mon Dieu*—it is good I have many sizes of the same shoes to match. Excellent, your feet have emerged. . . . Now we are back to our original position; now I pick up my saw and Tatiana screams, and you, Kadi, wriggle your feet—so—and with cries of terror I begin sawing."

Fiercely he sawed the boxes in two, accompanied by screams, until he slid the two boxes apart and the illusion was perfect: Tatiana's head remained at one end, presumably her feet wriggled at the opposite end, and between them there was only empty space.

Mrs. Pollifax laughed and applauded. "Bravo!"

"It is good? You see now?" asked the Professor, beaming.

"I see, yes. Tell Kadi I must go now," she called to him, and still chuckling she left them to their rehearsing and went out to find Willie.

Once again she sat across from Willie at his desk, this time to deliver her ultimatum. "I was tired last night," she told him, "and my thinking blurred but it is *not* blurred now. My husband will be returning to Connecticut on Monday from a meeting of the American Bar Association and I have every intention of being there when he comes home. If I'm to be of any help to you for a few days I need a great deal more information, for instance when your carnival opened and when this man Lazlo arrived here, and who might have come after he did, on the assumption that possibly he was followed here."

Willie leaned back in his chair and stared at her with distaste. "The police have just arrived to ask questions, and now you come to ask questions and speak of Bar Associations and such nonsense?"

"Yes," she said pleasantly. "Are you a Rom?"

"What?"

"Gypsy?"

His eyes glittered dangerously. "You ask—why?"

She shrugged. "You have the look. . . . I thought so last night, sleepy as I was," she said dryly. "I traveled once with gypsies in Europe."

"You?"

She nodded.

"Such a one as you?"

She smiled forgivingly. "Such a one as I, yes, and owe them my life."

He said scornfully, "This is hard to believe. What were the names of these people you profess to know—you, a *gajo*?"

"It was in Turkey. . . . There was Goru, and there was Sebastien and Orega, but most of all there was their Queen, a wonderful Zingari by the name of Anyeta Inglescu."

He stared at her, silent and frowning, and then with a nod he said brusquely, "I will get out my record book." Bringing it from a drawer of his desk he said, "We opened on March 1st in western Massachusetts, in the town of Lanesborough. We winter in Florida, still do a few dates in the South, strictly for Willie's Rich Uncle, you understand, but it's in the East they want us, and the carnival season always opens March 1st." He opened his record book. "Lazlo reached us in Vermont the second week of March, I was told to expect him. He came by bus, walking out to us from town."

"Not by helicopter?"

He looked amused. "We are not often so near such a big field to provide a quiet landing, and public airports are conspicuous, often watched, it can be difficult. I don't know why he came by bus, there must have been a reason because he walked in exhausted, with a broken arm."

"With a *what*?"

"A broken arm. We set it for him here, I've done it before. Gus and Pogo helped, and one of the roustabouts had been a paramedic." Consulting his book again he said, "But I remember we were not fully booked in the Ten-in-One when he came."

"You book everyone ahead of time?"

"Most," he said, nodding. "Most are regulars, very loyal, they come every season, the same three foremen and most of the acts and the roustabouts. Pogo and Gertie are the concession managers, I see they added a Spin the Wheel and a Cat-Rack game after Lazlo came. Those two, plus Jasna and her father and the Snake Woman came late. Lubo runs the Spin the Wheel, and Pie-Eye the Cat-Rack."

Mrs. Pollifax, fascinated by these names, said, "Then four arrived after Lazlo. But if Lazlo was followed here, surely it would be impossible for whoever located him to suddenly set up an act for a carnival?"

"Not so hard to set up a concession joint," he told her. "Anybody can do that, but harder for one of the Ten-in-One acts, they need talent. But," he added, "you're being naive, because anyone sent to me by

Willie's Rich Uncle is big-time, and whoever hunts him or her is big-time, too, and they need only snap a finger to find a killer."

"Even to find a killer who's a Snake Woman or knife-thrower?" she said dryly.

He smiled. "You'd be surprised, I'd be willing to bet the man who arranged your coming here—I name no names—could do the same." He returned to his list. "But it would need twenty-four hours at least to set something up, and all of these qualify. I had an ad running in Gibtown," he explained. "We lacked a couple more concessions and I had only six acts for the Ten-in-One. We take the leftovers, you see, the big expositions get the class acts. You take the Contortionist—his name's Norbert—he's a real class act but you'll notice he's too fond of the booze to make it anywhere but a gilly show like this."

"And the Snake Woman, and the Jasna act?"

He sighed. "Jasna's damn good with her knives but somebody may have realized her father's blind and figured it a bit nasty, her throwing knives at a blind man."

"Blind?"

Willie nodded. "Lost his sight some years ago, she said. Takes guts standing there and having knives thrown at him, and not even able to duck. As for the Snake Woman, I don't know."

"At least you've given me four names," Mrs. Pollifax said. "Anyone else?"

He shook his head, and leaning back in his chair looked her over thoughtfully. "You'll need good cover for asking questions I can't ask, and have no time to ask, anyway. A couple of years back in Vermont we had a feature writer from some newspaper spend a day with us—wrote a nice piece about how a carnival works. What about being here for the same purpose?"

"Oh, *much* better than fortune-telling," she agreed. "How soon can you get word around that last night's helicopter brought a newspaper writer to do interviews?"

He grinned. "If I tell Boozy Tim, word will get around fast enough. Incidentally, if anyone questions you at the gate tell them you're 'with it,' meaning with the carnie."

Mrs. Pollifax nodded and looked at her list:

Lubo/Spin the Wheel
Pie-Eye/Cat-Rack game
Jasna the Knife-thrower
The Snake Woman

"But if one of them had been planted here to kill Lazlo," she said with a frown, "wouldn't they have made a quick getaway?"

"Not *too* quick," he said. "With the police circulating it would have been conspicuous, not to mention suspicious. This would have been a clever killer, a pro, who chose just the right time—a crowd, nobody noticing. He or she would sit it out until the police leave."

She nodded and rose, and with a faint smile said,

"You changed your attitude toward me very suddenly, Willie, may I ask—?"

He grinned. "Oh, that." Showing her to the door he opened it for her. "I will tell you one day, but I will say now that the name of Inglescu is not unknown to me. Do you know the words in Rom '*ja develesa*'?"

She smiled. "Go with God?"

He nodded. "*Ja develesa,* then. And be careful."

CHAPTER 10

THE REPORT ON LAZLO HAD BEEN SENT down to Carstairs from Farnesworth's office, and it lay now on his desk in a neat little package that told him the conversation had been taped, for which he was grateful. Helga had put in her calls to France for him and had reached Desforges's residence successfully—he was having dinner with friends and was expected home by nine o'clock, European time. There was other work to do while Carstairs waited but he yielded to temptation and inserted the Lazlo tape in his machine, at the same time scanning Farnesworth's accompanying note: he had scrawled *What's up? Herewith Lazlo's phone call to me March 10, from Boston, where tailing a cash courier named Kopcha.*

The tape began.

"Yes, Lazlo here, calling from downtown, I may have been followed, I'm not sure. As scheduled, I had Kopcha under surveillance when he drove to a shell of a building half boarded up on a mean street, climbed the stairs and entered and after a minute I followed. He went into a third room, the only one with a door, and closed it behind him but there was a small foyer between the hallway and the door and I hid behind a pile of bricks to listen, God knows it looked safe enough with bricks to hide behind."

His voice, very controlled until now, trembled slightly. "What I heard was three men, two rough-talking but also a voice that spoke with authority, you know? Very smooth, with a French accent, I'm sure of this. They'd been expecting Kopcha and asked if he was interested in making some money on a big job, a cash pick-up—a ransom, they called it—in about a month's time. In April. They needed another man."

Farnesworth's voice, "Go on."

"Kopcha treated them with contempt, he was really arrogant. Wasn't interested in any small-time job, he told them scornfully, or working for a foreigner, and he walked out and left, followed by the others, which is when they found me behind the bricks, dragged me back into the room—the man with the French voice had disappeared—and they beat me up. Wanted to know how much, and what I'd heard, and who I was. I got away but one of them, for a couple of blocks, was behind me. Of course I lost Kopcha."

His voice broke. "I'm not feeling so well, I think my arm's broken."

The operator's voice broke in asking for more dimes and there was the sound of coins dropping into the slot.

Farnesworth said, "I'm hearing you, Lazlo. Two questions, fast. Any idea what you stumbled into?"

"Not a clue."

"What were these two men like, the two that beat you?"

"Nasty types. Looked just what Kopcha thought them, small fish with a small job. Shabby."

"And what do *you* think?"

There was hesitation before Lazlo spoke. "Not so sure of that, could be camouflage."

Again hesitation, and a sound of retching. "Sorry, I got hit in the gut, too. I thought maybe—I was at Willie's some years ago, would he be anywhere near Boston?"

"Best place for you," Farnesworth said, "Let's see where he is. . . . Hold on a minute. . . . Here we are, he's this week in Pownal, Vermont. But you sound in bad shape, Lazlo; if you can make it there fine, but go to a doctor first. I'll notify Willie to expect you."

"Yes."

And that was the end of the tape that had been recorded in March, one week after the carnival opened; now it was April and Willie was in Maine. *Poor devil,* thought Carstairs, *he escaped from that situa-*

tion with a broken arm, only to have a knife plunged into his back weeks later. It *could* be assumed that he was careless in making his way to Vermont in March, but Carstairs fervently hoped this wasn't the case because he didn't want to consider the possibility of losing Willie's Traveling Show as a safe house.

On the other hand, he reflected, leaning back in his chair and frowning, if Lazlo had been followed that craftily, that successfully, and for such a distance, it implied that what he had stumbled into on March 10th—what Kopcha had dismissed so casually, and Lazlo, too—was a hell of a lot more important than either of them realized.

Judiciously he considered Lazlo, born Aziz Kalad, a very experienced and dedicated agent who had spent four years undercover in Iran, risking his life to survive and to smuggle out information. Hard to believe that he wouldn't cover his tracks, and then Carstairs amended this as he recalled the sound of retching and of nerves gone hellishly ragged. *Burnout,* he mused; a broken arm, probably a high temperature—yes, they should have insisted he take a vacation. He *could* have become careless in the route he'd chosen two months ago to reach Willie in Vermont.

He switched on the machine and played the tape again, this time curious about the job Kopcha had been offered. The word ransom interested him, as did the reference to "next month. In April." It was next month now, and the word ransom loomed very large in the news.

Helga's voice interrupted his thoughts and brought him back to the present moment. "Your call to France has come through, sir, Mr. Desforges is on line three."

With an effort, Carstairs removed his thoughts from Lazlo to concentrate them on the country of Ubangiba and a geophysicist named Rogere Desforges.

"Monsieur Desforges?" he began.

The man had a pleasant voice, and once Carstairs had introduced himself Desforges shifted easily into English with only a faint accent.

Carstairs drew a deep breath. He had the advantage of the man at the opposite end of the line: he knew precisely what he wanted to ask, and he knew the skill with which he must question him, but it held all the elements of a surgical operation with the risk of hitting a wrong nerve and killing communication. "You're aware," he said gently, "that Henry Bidwell has been abducted in the United States?"

"Yes, I've seen something of it in the newspapers here. Most tragic!"

Carstairs said carefully, "In our attempts to find out if he had provoked interest from some foreign group we'd be interested in learning of your visit to Ubangiba with him." He waited, poised for disappointment, braced for word that Desforges's only connection with Bidwell had occurred in Paris, and that he'd never seen Ubangiba.

With infinite relief and a sense of triumph he heard Desforges say easily, "Oh yes, that was certainly interesting. I must say, those African potentates live well. *Most* interesting."

Carstairs, in an attempt to decipher just what this meant, hazarded an amused, "Well entertained, were you?"

"*Mon Dieu,* yes! Champagne, pheasant, caviar, all the good things of life."

Carstairs, hopes rising, continued, "You would say, then, that Bidwell had established a congenial relationship with the President?"

"Definitely, yes. Old friends, one might say. We stayed at the palace two of the nights, and when we went out into the field we had escorts and guards. Very well taken care of. Of course the people are starving," he added ruefully, "while the President is designing a third palace and having all his caviar flown in from Europe. One regrets this sort of thing but business was business in Bidwell's case."

"Of course," Carstairs said, and, "What *was* the nature of his business, Monsieur Desforges?"

"That, I am not at liberty to tell you, of course, without Bidwell's consent."

"As you know," Carstairs said crisply, "this is Central Intelligence calling. Perhaps if your *Sûreté* asked the question?"

Desforges hesitated. "I would have to say the same to them, you know. Client confidentiality and all that." He added cautiously, "It is perhaps permissible to say that Monsieur Bidwell and his company now own exclusive mineral rights to the country."

"Oh yes," Carstairs murmured noncommittally. "Do you happen to recall the name of the company?"

"Offhand, no, I only glimpsed it on documents."

"Would it be Claiborne-Osborne International?"

"No, no, quite different, Something-Something Mining Company of Ubangiba, but I don't recall the attached name."

Aha, thought Carstairs, and risked another wild guess. "With Lecler and Romanovitch involved, of course."

"Yes, their names were mentioned."

Better and better, thought Carstairs, there was beginning to be a shape to this. "Thank you, Monsieur Desforges," he said, and as if just thinking of this he added, "Oh—one last question, if I may ask it without endangering your—uh—client confidentiality. Would you say that from a business point of view their acquiring the mineral rights will prove profitable?"

"Hmmmm," murmured Desforges thoughtfully. "Of course oil or natural gas would be far more profitable but I suppose any form of energy in that region . . . With cheap labor, and it would have to be *very* cheap labor—a bit Leopoldish, of course—but with cheap labor profitable, yes."

Carstairs felt a rush of excitement; Bidwell might not have struck oil but he felt that he had struck it. "Thank you, Monsieur Desforges," he said with conviction.

Energy, he reflected, and rang the Africa section; it was time to find out what, if anything, Bidwell planned for Ubangiba. "Allan?" he said. "Carstairs here. I want to learn what your geology department can find out from the various strata—what I think are called the metamorphic and sedimentary rock formations?—of the country of Ubangiba. I want to know just what minerals could possibly be unearthed there. Not known, you understand, but potential."

"What do you mean, not known?" asked Allan.

"Just that. So far as the usual descriptions of the country go, there are no minerals at all. On the other hand, someone seems to have discovered something that's made it worth tying up exclusive mineral rights over there and I gather it's neither oil nor natural gas."

"Hmmm," murmured Allan. "Tin, gold, iron-ore, wolfram . . ."

rstairs shook his head. "It's been referred to as energy-producing but not oil."

"That'll take a few days," said Allan. "We'll have to start from scratch with an analysis, and do some real research."

"That's expected," Carstairs told him. "As soon as possible, though, and with my thanks."

He glanced up as Bishop walked into his office.

"I'm back," said Bishop gloomily. "Raining in New York and my trip was a wild goose chase, wasn't it? A total waste?"

"Not at all," Carstairs assured him smoothly, and with a glance at his watch, "Nearly four o'clock, you've not had time to connect with Mrs. Pollifax, I suppose?"

"No rest for the weary," sighed Bishop. "I'll try right now but Willie seldom inhabits his office afternoons. He does, however, have an answering machine so I'll just keep calling and leaving messages. That should annoy him."

"Do that," said Carstairs, turning to the work on his desk. "She's safe, which is what matters, but I'd like to know why on earth she needed a safe house here in the United States when not on any assignment. Keep trying."

CHAPTER 11

KADI WAS HAVING THE TIME OF HER LIFE. After all, she had never been sawed in half before, and in concentrating on the Professor's instructions and listening for the key words that would tell her the moment when she and Tatiana would be spun dizzily in a wide circle, she completely forgot her two days in a closet, Chigi Scap Metal, and her anxieties about Sammy. She had entered a world of magic and drama, and after a very sobering adolescence she was experiencing playtime. It was surprising how restful it felt, and how liberating.

By two o'clock the Professor announced that she had mastered the timing of her role in the act and that she could be released to investigate her startling new environment. Before she left he delved into a trunk in the rear and handed her a pair of black stockings and a pair of size 5 shoes that matched Tatiana's. "Take 'em along and be back here six o'clock sharp."

Kadi went at once to the trailer to rummage through her knapsack for the sketchbooks she'd taken to New Haven in what felt now an eternity ago. A carnival, she thought, would be a wonderful opportunity for sketching faces.

She found Mrs. Pollifax already in the trailer with a notepad in her lap. "I'm to be a feature writer for a newspaper and interview some of the carnies," she told Kadi. "I have narrowly escaped being a fortune-teller."

Abruptly Kadi sat down, knapsack on her lap. "Mrs. Pollifax—"

"It's Mrs. Reed," she reminded her pleasantly.

"Reed . . . Reed," said Kadi, "but why? And—you said you would explain, didn't you? To be here of all places, and suddenly you're not Mrs. Polli—I mean, suddenly you're Mrs. *Reed*."

Mrs. Pollifax nodded. "Yes, I suppose you have to know. . . ." Leaving her bunk to sit beside Kadi she said, "You understand this is *very* confidential."

"Yes," Kadi said, watching her face.

Keeping her voice low, "You've heard of the Central Intelligence Agency in this country, the CIA?" Kadi nodded. "Some years ago, during a difficult time in my life"—she smiled, remembering—"I applied for work with them, quite outrageously, of course, but also out of desperation because I'd come to a dead end in my life. The man who interviewed me—I can't describe how shocked he was—wanted to get rid of me as fast as possible, but by chance I was seen by a man who was looking for someone just like me and thought I'd be an excellent courier. An Innocent Tourist, he called me.

"I barely survived *that* mission," she told Kadi dryly, "but it ended successfully and since then I've been given other assignments abroad. So you see, when I found you in my closet I was—well, somewhat experienced in surprises, and when I made my phone call from the hospital it was to someone I know in the—the *Department*."

Kadi, watching her wide-eyed, said shakily, "You mean I picked just the perfect person to help me."

"Not perfect," Mrs. Pollifax said modestly, "but not uninitiated. The surprise for me is that this carnival is semi-supported by my—er—friends, as a place where people in danger are occasionally sent by the Department for safekeeping. Willie told me this last night. It's assumed that Willie's Rich Uncle bails out the carnival when it can't pay its bills, which I have to say is tremendously inventive and clever. But one of the men sent by Willie's Rich Uncle was knifed last night while we were flying here and I've been asked to help. *Only* for a few days," she added firmly.

"Wow," said Kadi admiringly. "Can I help, too?"

Mrs. Pollifax smiled. "You can help by remembering to call me Emmy, or Mrs. Reed, and by noticing anything odd here. Except," she added reasonably, "I expect that *everything* will seem rather odd to us. For instance—" She glanced at her list, "I am now going to try and locate a Snake Woman. What do you plan to do?"

"Sketch people," said Kadi. "For practice."

Mrs. Pollifax looked at her thoughtfully. "A very good idea. Of course a few here may object to being sketched. . . . Perhaps you could explain that Willie's trying you out for a concession of your own. Sketching people."

Kadi leaned over and kissed her on the cheek. "I do admire the way your mind works."

"And if anyone questions you, say you're 'with it,' " added Mrs. Pollifax.

"With what?"

"I suppose with the carnival; it's what one says, or so Willie told me. To tell them you belong."

"Belong," said Kadi wistfully. "What a nice word," and opening the door she walked out, sketchbook and pen in hand, to explore the midway.

Mrs. Pollifax found a match and burned her small list of carnival suspects and then ventured out herself. It was past three o'clock and as she left the circle of trailers and entered the midway she saw a police car parked near the big tent called the Ten-in-One. A policeman was standing beside it. Mrs. Pollifax's glance veered to the right as a second policeman ushered out of the tent an extremely odd-looking young person carrying, in outstretched arms like a libation, a gleaming mahogany box. Mrs.

Pollifax slowed her pace, not sure whether the policeman was escorting a young woman or a young boy: he or she was thin as a reed, and tall, with a shock of orange hair clipped in the style referred to as punk, wearing a pink halter tight as a Band-Aid across the chest, and tight black slacks. Only when her eyes fell to the high-heeled shoes, and at last noted two small bulges under the halter did she realize it was a young woman. Her face was no less startling than her tall thin body: thin sharp features and a bright slash of scarlet lips.

"She's got her knives, Lieutenant," the policeman called to his companion. "Very different ones, no similarity."

"Let's see," the lieutenant said. "You're Jasna?"

The young woman nodded and placed the mahogany box on the hood of the car. Opening it, she said in a lightly accented voice, "These I work with. The case stays locked. It is locked *always* until my act begins."

Mrs. Pollifax, lingering in the shadow of a booth, watched the lieutenant bring out a tape measure, pluck one of the long pointed knives from the box and measure it. "You throw these? At a man?"

She nodded indifferently. "Yes."

"You never miss? He doesn't mind?"

"He taught me," she said with a shrug. "Before that it was I who stood on the platform and he who threw the knives."

From between two concession booths a bearded man appeared, wearing a long cape, his head tilted up, eyes concealed by dark glasses. "Jasna?" he called. "Jasna?"

"Over here, Papa," she called out to him.

As he took a few steps forward he prodded the earth with a cane, and Mrs. Pollifax realized that he was the blind man that Willie had mentioned last night. The two policemen watching his progress looked shocked. "Good God, blind," murmured the lieutenant.

"If you must know, yes," the girl said coldly, "but once, in Europe, he was famous before he lost his sight." To the old man she said, "It's all right, Papa, they only wanted to see the knives, see if one had been stolen, or if I—" She gave the two men an amused glance, "If I went about trying to kill people."

Her father's cane found the car and he stopped, his cane as alive as fingers searching for Jasna. "Over here, Papa," she said softly. "Now—you have seen the knives, we can go?"

The lieutenant brought a photograph from his pocket. "From the depth and width of the wound it would have been a knife like this," he said, handing the photograph to her. "Ever seen one of *these* knives?"

She said scornfully, "It looks like a kitchen knife, you would do better to ask in the cook-house."

"I'd call it a dagger," the lieutenant said.

She said with a shrug, "Not one of mine."

Mrs. Pollifax decided to move along before she was seen, and slipping through the space from which

Jasna's father had entered the midway she walked around the back of the Ten-in-One and came out farther down the midway. Several of the booths were open now and occupied, with their flaps rolled up; at one of them a man on a ladder was touching up a sign with a paint brush while Kadi was standing at another booth arguing with the man behind the counter. As Mrs. Pollifax neared her she heard Kadi say, "I told you I'm 'with it' but I'll pay, I will if you want. All you have to do is start the ducks moving, I don't even want a prize."

She was facing a ruddy-faced man with a stubborn mouth who glared at her angrily. "You nag worse than my wife . . . nag nag nag," he growled. "To get rid of you—okay once, just once, you hear? Then *scram*."

Mrs. Pollifax stopped behind her. It was a shooting gallery that had caught Kadi's attention, a few rifles in a row on the counter and a line of yellow ducks in suspension along the back wall. With a martyred sigh the man pressed a button and the ducks began moving; he continued to glare at Kadi, who picked up one of the B-B guns, aimed, fired rapidly, and knocked over all eight of the moving ducks.

Beaming, Kadi thanked him. "That was great fun, thanks, really."

Mrs. Pollifax, staring at her in surprise, was not alone in her reaction.

"Hey girlie," shouted the man, "come back."

Kadi turned.

"Can you do that again?"

"Well, I suppose so," Kadi said, considering this.

"Even faster? Show me." He pressed the button and the ducks flew upright again and began moving across the back panel, but faster now. Kadi lifted a rifle, aimed, fired, and seven of the eight fell over. He stared at her. "Look, kid," he said, "you wanna work for me tonight? You be my stick and I'll pay you, it'll bring in the marks like bees to honey."

"What's a stick?" asked Kadi.

"The come-on . . . the tip sees how easy a kid like you shoots down the ducks, they can't wait to get out their wallets." He winked. "At least until they win too much." He didn't explain what he did if they won too much.

Kadi said politely, "Thank you very much but I've got a job with the Professor, I'm being sawed in half."

He leaned forward eagerly. "Look, any time you're between acts, you come here, I'd appreciate that, young lady. Name's Pogo." He thrust out a calloused hand to shake, and Kadi politely extended hers, shook it and said, "I'll see, Pogo. Thanks."

Turning and seeing Mrs. Pollifax, she grinned. "Hello, Emmy Reed!"

"Kadi," said Mrs. Pollifax in awe, "where on earth did you learn to shoot like that?"

"Oh, at home in Ubangiba," she said, joining her. "Sand grouse and scorpions and snakes—Sammy and Rabi and Duma and me. I had only a B-B gun but Sammy and Duma had real pistols."

"You certainly won Pogo's heart." Mrs. Pollifax

glanced down at the sketchbook Kadi carried tucked under her arm. "I see you've already sketched him."

Kadi laughed. "Well, it's mostly a caricature, there wasn't much time."

"But I recognize him at once," said Mrs. Pollifax, studying the quick sketch. "That protruding underlip—and that's a very witty line suggesting his broken nose. Have you done others?"

Kadi stopped and turned a page. "Just this."

"Jasna!" exclaimed Mrs. Pollifax. "Perfect! I've just seen her." Smiling, she said, "I'll have to write the New Haven police department and tell them what a terrible mistake they made, not hiring you."

"I wish you would," Kadi said wistfully. "I really need a job."

"You just had an offer," pointed out Mrs. Pollifax with a twinkle.

Kadi laughed. "I did, didn't I."

Willie was striding down the midway, looking harassed, but seeing them he stopped. "Go all right with the Professor?" he asked Kadi.

"Oh yes," she said eagerly, "but Mr. Willie, how did you know my name was African?"

He grinned. "Rule one in a carnival: never ask personal questions. So I'll ask you one: what country you from?"

"Ubangiba."

He nodded. "Know any pidgin English?"

She laughed. "A little. *Gut ifnin, ha yu de?*"

"A de wel," he said, laughing with her. *"A de fayn."*

"Gut," she told him. *"Waka fayn."*

MORE dimensions to this man, thought Mrs. Pollifax; *it suggests a good many adventures for the CIA in his youth.* She said, "I'm sorry to interrupt, but where will I find the Snake Woman, Willie?"

He glanced at his watch. "Still in her trailer. Dark brown mobile home, red curtains," and to Kadi, with a smile, *"Waka fayn,"* and strode away.

She left Kadi staring after Willie with a look of amazement and pleasure on her face, and made her exit from the midway, giving the police car a surreptitious glance and noting that it was empty. Reaching the circle of trailers she located the dark brown mobile home, as long and luxurious as Willie's. An extremely voluptuous young woman was sunning herself in a lawn chair near it, and seeing Mrs. Pollifax she called out with a friendly smile, "Come say hello, you're the lady going to get us in the newspaper, right?"

Startled, Mrs. Pollifax said, "But how did you know?"

The girl laughed. "Boozy Tim told me, Boozy Tim knows all the gossip, he knows *everything* that goes on here. Have a seat." A hand with brilliant red nails indicated the chair next to her.

Mrs. Pollifax made a mental note to look up this Boozy Tim who "knew everything," but she resisted the invitation. "I'm looking for the Snake Woman, are you—?"

"Oh, her . . . she's feeding her snakes just now."

The hand was casually waved toward the trailer behind her. "I'd advise waiting, it's a messy business."

Mrs. Pollifax eyed the mass of brown hair in the girl's lap. "Is that alive?"

"Lord no," she said, laughing. "It's my wig, honey, I was brushing it." She held it up to her head to display long corkscrew curls that reached to her waist. "I'm half the girlie show, me and Zilka. Shannon Summer's the name. Sit."

Mrs. Pollifax sat. She also stared, for there was a great deal of Shannon Summer at which to stare, six feet of her at least, with long legs and curves that appeared to defy every law of nature, topped off with a saucy round face and wide smile. "Girlie show?" she said.

"Yeah, just bumps and grinds, they're real strict in this state. Anywhere these days, mostly."

"With that figure," said Mrs. Pollifax frankly, "I should think you'd be in show business. Broadway, I mean. Aren't you wasted on a carnival?"

Shannon Summer laughed contentedly. "Oh, this is the life for me, I like to move. . . . Move move move is my motto. I got booked once in a revue in New York, and staying in one place drove me crazy. Besides, I got lonesome. This is like family."

Struck by what she said, Mrs. Pollifax realized that she ought to be writing it down, and brought out notebook and pen.

"Do I get my picture in the papers?" asked Shannon.

Mrs. Pollifax found herself embarrassed at telling

a blatant untruth but she said smoothly, "Probably, yes, but not until the last day I'm here; he can't be spared until then."

"Here only one day?" pouted Shannon. "Honey, you can bet your aunt's fanny it'll rain. Is he good looking?"

"I'm sure of it," Mrs. Pollifax told her, fingers crossed.

"Good. Are the fuzz—police—still poking around?"

"Their car's still parked on the midway."

Shannon's eyes turned mournful. "Pretty tough on that guy Lazlo. Frankly I never seen him until he was on that stretcher. Hi, Boozy Tim," she called.

Mrs. Pollifax turned to meet Boozy Tim and couldn't help but smile. He was a toothless, wizened, joyful little man wearing a baseball cap set at a jaunty angle. He grinned and tipped his cap to her.

"Boozy Tim," said Shannon with authority, "has met God."

"I beg your pardon?" said Mrs. Pollifax.

"Yes ma'am," said Boozy Tim, twinkling at her. "Met with God. He come to me—me, Boozy Tim. Talked to me, too."

"Tell her," Shannon said. "Tell her."

Boozy Tim nudged his way onto the arm of Shannon's chair and lifted his arms dramatically. "He come to me all gold, a gold cloud, like how things look on a misty day, fuzzy, you know? and shimmering all over. And he lifted his arms to me—" He nodded eagerly. "Like this. And he told me things."

"Private things," Shannon announced, nodding.

"Yes ma'am. And I never took a drop of liquor again, no need for it after *that*."

"No," whispered Mrs. Pollifax, mesmerized by the radiance of him as he spoke. "Not after *that*."

He pointed a finger at her. "You're Emmy Reed," he said, and winked at her. "Come to make a story about us."

She admitted to this, wondering what his wink meant, and if he knew very well that she was an impostor. Shannon had said "he knows everything" and perhaps he did, but she could only return his delighted smile without skepticism: how else, she wondered, could one respond to such a happy little man? "I'd better be about my business," she said, rising, "but I feel very privileged to have met you, Boozy Tim, and perhaps—perhaps we can talk again later?"

"Yes ma'am," he said, beaming at her. "Pleased to meet you." He tipped his hat again as she left them to head for the Snake Woman's trailer, hoping the snakes had now been fed their rats or mice, or whatever it was that gave snakes pleasure. She had lifted her hand to knock on the closed door when a buzz of electronic static interrupted the calm of the afternoon and a loudspeaker sprang into life.

A harsh voice battled the static to say, "This is Willie here. . . . No tear-down tomorrow, the police won't let us go. Not anybody, not until they finish their investigation. A hell of a bad show for us, but there it is. . . ."

A smoother voice followed: "This is Detective-Lieutenant Allbright to say we are sorry for this inconvenience. However," he explained firmly, "we can't allow you to move on to a town sixty miles away until our investigation into the near-murder of one of your people has been completed. Anybody leaving will be stopped and arrested. Thank you."

Behind her Mrs. Pollifax heard Shannon say, "What the hell's going on? A roustabout gets hurt and the fuzz never care, and what about Willie? Posters out, the next lot rented and pegged, the squeeze fixed by the patch . . ."

Mrs. Pollifax shook her head with a smile at this new vocabulary and knocked on the door facing her. She could hear voices arguing; she knocked again.

The door was flung open by an angry, dark young man with black hair and mustache. Behind him Mrs. Pollifax glimpsed a faded blonde woman who shouted at him, "I *told* you we should have left last night, I *told* you—"

Mrs. Pollifax said politely, "How do you do, I'm—"

She was not allowed to finish. The man said, "Sorry, lady, we're leaving. . . . Throw me the keys, Elda—*keys*."

A set of keys flew through the air, and gripping them he slammed the door behind him and raced to the cab that pulled the trailer. Mrs. Pollifax retreated as the motor roared, the trailer backed a few feet, moved out of the circle and tore off across the field, bouncing over ruts and hillocks.

Obviously it was the police announcement that had sent the Snake Woman and her companion in full flight, which in itself, thought Mrs. Pollifax, was certainly very interesting. She wondered if they would succeed in making their escape over the fields or if the police had anticipated just such a move before the announcement. In any case the Snake Woman had just earned an asterisk beside her name on the list that Willie had given her, and Mrs. Pollifax set out to find the Spin the Wheel booth and to see whether its proprietor Lubo would earn an asterisk, too, or just a plain check beside his name.

CHAPTER 12

CROSSING THE MIDWAY, MRS. POLLIFAX noticed Willie talking sternly to Boozy Tim next to the transformer; when she glanced back the two men were just disappearing into Willie's trailer. More booths—or joints, as Willie called them—had begun opening up as the afternoon progressed; the man painting his sign was climbing down from his ladder, and she was relieved to see that farther down the midway Lubo's Spin the Wheel was unshuttered and occupied. The booth was difficult to miss: a flashy banner shouted SPIN THE ARROW! VALUABLE PRIZES VALUABLE! and somewhat smaller but in no less garish colors: *Win a TV! Win a VCR! FUN FUN FUN!*

The man behind the counter didn't look fun at all;

she guessed him to be in his thirties, with a face as still as a pool of unruffled water. Not expressionless, she decided, but guarded and watchful, and the dark eyes that lifted as she neared him were so piercing they produced the effect of an electrical shock: she felt measured, analyzed, X-rayed, categorized, and all this with a riveting stillness that was unnerving. She wondered if they were the eyes of a Mephistopheles, a mystic, or a murderer.

"You must be Lubo," she said cheerfully. "Willie's given me permission to spend a few days with the carnival, I'm doing a feature story for my newspaper."

"What paper?" he asked abruptly.

"Portland *Gazette*," she fired back.

"Never heard of it."

Nor had she, but to match his machine-gun style of shooting out words she said crisply, "It's new."

A tight perfunctory smile twitched the corners of his mouth; she doubted that he believed her. "So?"

Notebook in hand she said, "So I'd like to ask how long you've been working in carnivals, Mr. Lubo, and has it always been with Spin the Wheel? And do you enjoy the life?"

He shrugged. "Don't know yet."

"That new?"

"That new."

She smiled politely. "What made you decide to join Willie's Traveling Show?"

"Needed work." His eyes were studying her with an intensity that made her uncomfortable.

She scribbled a few words, nodding. "Interesting . . . May I ask what line of work you were in before?"

Without expression he said, "No."

"You're not exactly giving me feature-story material," she told him frankly, meeting his eyes, and with a pleasant smile added, "Not exactly forthcoming, are you?"

"No," he said.

She nodded. "Thanks anyway," and walked away, still scribbling on her notepad but adding now: Lubo, cultured voice, intelligent, expensive-looking Rolex watch, new at carnivals, not precisely hostile but definitely neither communicative nor friendly. Eyes a bit scary.

The Cat-Rack booth was still closed. As she returned to her trailer she saw that the Snake Woman's long brown mobile home was in place again, ignominiously turned back by the police, apparently, and its red curtains tightly drawn as if to close out the world. *Not* an auspicious moment for an interview, decided Mrs. Pollifax, and continued on to the trailer that she and Kadi shared.

She found Kadi crouched on her bunk trying on the black stockings and shoes for the six o'clock opening. "They pinch," she said, taking a few steps in the shoes. "But aren't they pretty?"

"Yes indeed, and at least you needn't walk in them," pointed out Mrs. Pollifax. "Do more sketching? I was wondering if you remember enough of Sammy's roommate to sketch him for me, and Sammy, too."

Kadi smiled. "I don't have to sketch Sammy, I've a snapshot of him." Reaching into her knapsack she pulled out a wallet and then a photograph. "Here's Sammy."

It was a group snapshot, taken under a hot sun: three black faces, three white. Kadi said, "That's my mother and father—and Rakia, the head nurse, and Tiamoko, my dad's assistant—and me—and that's Sammy at the far end."

Obviously it had been taken some years ago; Kadi looked fourteen or fifteen at most, and very small next to Sammy, who was a sturdy and attractive teenager with a broad smile on his face, but she found herself more interested in Kadi's parents. They stood in front of a shadeless cement-block building with a sign that read: MANKHWALA NYUMBA. "What does that mean?" she asked, pointing.

"Medicine house."

"Why were they shot, Kadi?" she asked gently.

Her face totally without expression, Kadi said, "Because someone betrayed them, they were accused of helping too much the people wanting change, they were shot as spies."

Yes, they would have helped, thought Mrs. Pollifax, studying the two of them: Mrs. Hopkirk with her plain strong face, Dr. Hopkirk erect, reserved, with eyes and brows that matched Kadi's. Never for them the easy life or the easy choice, by the look of them and their surroundings, but it was Kadi who must be protected now.

When she handed back the photograph she noticed

that Kadi didn't look at it again—or dared not. "Thank you," she told her with a smile. "And now it's surely time for early dinner, isn't it? I intend to try one of those 'biggest hotdogs in the USA'—how about it?"

"Oh, *yes,*" Kadi said, and they headed companionably to the grab-joint.

At six o'clock Mrs. Pollifax stood in the field outside the entrance and watched the carnival spring into life. Over the ticket booth loomed a proscenium on which spotlights played across giant words proclaiming WILLIE'S TRAVELING SHOW OF FUN AND MIRTH, *Games! Prizes! Rides! Shows!* Behind her the field was filling with cars and trucks, and people—*townies,* she remembered—were pouring in, abandoning for this night their televisions and VCRs to see live entertainment. On the platform next to the entrance the talker was shouting, "Hully, hully, hully . . . a world of treats for you tonight, folks. Two lush and beautiful gals straight from Paris, France, do the Dance of the Seven Veils that'll knock your eyes out, I can tell you! And Elda the Snake Woman with her ten live and dangerous snakes you won't see anywhere but here at Willie's . . . and don't miss Jasna the Knife-thrower—she might miss tonight, ladies and gentlemen, she might miss!"

His booming voice was supplanted by others as Mrs. Pollifax walked past the ticket booth, confiding that she was "with it," and proceeded onto the midway, braced against the waves of sound that had blossomed all at once to transform the midway into a promise of adventure and excitement. The ferris wheel had begun turning, the thumping music of the merry-go-round formed a backdrop to lighten the heart, and passing the concessions the voices competed in mounting volume for attention . . . "Hey, mister . . . Hey, pretty girl! . . . Hey, tall guy . . . step right up, ladies, try your luck! Cotton candy here, cotton candy here . . . !"

And somewhere among these people, she reminded herself, was a would-be murderer, unless Lazlo's attacker had walked through those same gates, cleverly drawn a crowd, and dashed away as soon as the deed was done. A possibility, conceded Mrs. Pollifax, but surely with so many carnies at work it would have needed more than one visit to the carnival to locate this Lazlo who had quietly collected tickets at the merry-go-round. Willie, encountered earlier on the midway, reported the police had already checked the three motels in the area and had found one traveling salesman who had not left his motel at night, and three families with small children. In these small towns strangers were noticed, and motels had few guests in April. If Lazlo was important enough to have been tucked away here by the Department, she thought it more likely the carnival had been infiltrated—there was that "Hey Rube," for instance—and whoever "they" were, they would not have been careless; there would have been a plan worked out to precisely fit the circumstances.

And the circumstances at a carnival, she thought wryly, were exotic and surely daunting.

What she refused to consider was the carnival's cover being blown as a safe house; she couldn't bear to think of all these people losing their jobs and Willie his traveling show.

I'm becoming hooked, she thought with a smile.

Pogo's shooting gallery already had a cluster of young men and boys around it. As she passed Lubo and his Spin the Wheel she slowed, and then stopped to admire his technique: he was still the same Lubo, speaking with rapid-fire crispness into his microphone but softly, in a low voice, and so confidentially that passersby stopped to hear what he was saying. "The odds are eight to one," he was almost whispering into his mike. "Try the wheel, beat the odds, I dare you . . . Mathematically you'll find this game is . . ."

She walked on, wondering if Lubo could be the one. She would do what she could for Willie, at least until Cyrus came home and until Kadi was safe, but she saw no likelihood of unearthing a suspect in only a few days. She could readily understand that Willie had no time to prowl about and investigate, whereas she was free to wander and observe, but she was also a stranger to these people. She might, of course, be less threatening to them than the police, who had been circulating all day; they were still here, but less obtrusively; she had noticed one of their cars parked behind the trailers not far from where the helicopter had landed and she supposed a few plainclothesmen might be roaming the midway.

The Ten-in-One was just opening and a tall thin man was testing the microphone on the bally platform. She stopped, eager to see Kadi's performance no matter how invisibly she performed. The talker cleared his throat, called out, "Over here, friends, step this way, folks!" and began describing the delights awaiting them in the side-show tent. To emphasize this, Shannon and Zilka made their entrance on the platform to a flurry of shrill whistles; they were all legs and long hair, with everything in between scanty, sequined, and glittering. El Flamo joined them brandishing a flaming torch, followed by the Professor and Tatiana, her red hair set off by black tights. Last of all came the Snake Woman, so ignominiously returned to Willie's by the police. She was introduced with one huge snake in her arms and another wrapped around her neck. *Brave woman,* thought Mrs. Pollifax, looking at her closely, but not a happy one, she decided: not even the heavy eye make-up could quite distract from the anxious, haunted expression in her eyes. *Going on forty,* summed up Mrs. Pollifax: faded blonde hair badly curled and lips too red. Only when she held up one of the snakes did her face change, become tender and younger as if the snake in her hands gave her more contentment than any human.

Mrs. Pollifax walked inside, and for the ensuing thirty-five minutes she watched as Jasna coolly aimed and threw her long and deadly knives at her father standing against a distant backboard; saw the Snake Woman talk to her snakes, play with them, give a running commentary about them, heard them hiss alarmingly, and appreciated her finale when she draped all ten snakes around her. She watched the Professor draw eggs out of a hat and rainbow-colored scarves out of his ear, and she was pleased to see that he successfully sawed Tatiana and Kadi in half.

It was following this that she found Boozy Tim standing beside her. He said, "Willie tole me I should talk to you now."

"Oh, good," she said, "I've been wanting to talk to you, too, you know so much and I so little."

"Yes'm," he said, beaming at her. "Happen to know why you're here, and mum's the word."

Leaving the midway they moved into the shadows back of one of the booths, where she turned to face him. "Boozy Tim, can you tell me anything about last night? Were you in the crowd when the man was knifed?"

"Yes'm," he said, nodding.

"Anywhere near?"

"Yes'm."

"Did you notice anything? See any of it? See anyone *near* Lazlo when it happened?"

Boozy Tim sighed. "Well, like I tole Willie—he had me in his office this afternoon—I didn't see anything *really*, except—"

She said quickly, "Except?"

He made a face. "Just a man with a white beard,

like I tole Willie. Wouldn't have noticed him at all except he stepped on my foot. Never saw his face but—" He frowned, puzzled. "Something familiar about him. *Something.*"

"Like what?" she asked.

He hesitated. "Don't rightly know, Emmy. Just saw the beard as he turned sideways, away from me. Didn't see his *face*. Maybe the way he held his shoulders. Or his nose. Or his head, maybe."

"What was he wearing?"

He shook his head. "Wasn't much light down there, all those people squeezed in a huddle. Dressed like a townie, I'd say, black sweater, black wind-breaker. Only saw him quick—sideways, and then his back."

"He didn't apologize for stepping on your foot?"

Boozy Tim shook his head. "In a hurry. No."

In a hurry . . . "You told Willie this?"

"Yep, except I didn't think of it right away."

"Did you notice anyone else near Lazlo?"

Again he shook his head. "Didn't even know Lazlo was up ahead of me 'til he just sunk to the ground and somebody screamed."

"Who screamed?" she asked.

"Lady who runs the hanky panky near the gate—she come over to see what the 'Hey Rube' was all about, excepting there warn't no reason for any 'Hey Rube' at all, it turned out."

"And Willie knows this? You've told him?"

"Oh yes, ma'am. But there's nobody here in Willie's show with a white beard. White as Santa Claus's beard, pure white like snow. Nobody here like that."

"I see," she said, frowning. "How old would you have guessed the man to be, the one who was in a hurry to leave, and stepped on your foot?"

Boozy Tim considered this judiciously. "Can't say, but he moved pretty damn fast for a man with a white beard."

"Do you think the beard was false?" she asked. "A disguise?"

This had apparently not occurred to him and he looked troubled. "Only saw it fast," he said. "Real fast, and never thought about it anyway 'til Willie asked and *asked* if I'd noticed anybody up near Lazlo. Hear he's still alive, is that right?"

"So far as I know," said Mrs. Pollifax, frowning over his story.

"Willie really grilled me," Boozy Tim said. "He tole me 'Boozy Tim, if you was there you *seen* things' and I said 'no, Willie, didn't see a thing.' But then my foot was hurtin' and all that—still hurts a little—so I remembered *that*, and tole him."

"Thank you," she said gravely, and smiled at him. "You must be a great help to Willie, do you run a concession?"

"Me?" He grinned his broad toothless smile. "Oh no, ma'am, I repair what breaks down. Not much I don't know about the pig-iron—rides, that is—when they stop runnin'. Mechanic, that's me," he said with pride.

Mrs. Pollifax smiled back at him. "I like you, Boozy Tim."

"Like you, too," he said in a pleased voice. "Gotta check the merry-go-round, want a ride?"

"*Love* one."

"I give 'em all names," he confided. "You ride on Cynthia, she's my favorite."

In this manner Mrs. Pollifax ended her first carnival evening riding dreamily up and down on Cynthia, lights flashing, the calliope playing "In the Good Old Summertime." She would have preferred to imagine herself riding to the rescue of the cavalry, or across a great desert to meet a sheikh who would definitely resemble Cyrus, but her mind remained fixed on a man who had stepped on Boozy Tim's foot in his hurry to leave the crowd last night, when people usually moved closer to learn what had caused a woman to scream.

CHAPTER 13

ON FRIDAY MORNING BISHOP ARRIVED IN his office fifteen minutes late. "Sorry," he apologized, "but I ran into the FBI at the café where I eat breakfast every morning . . . you know, Jed Addams. Want to hear the latest news on the Bidwell abduction?"

"Is anyone immune?" said Carstairs dryly. "What's been happening?"

"Strictly hush-hush, of course, but Jed says there have been three aborted attempts at delivering the ransom—three, no less, in one week. They put together the fifty million in unmarked bills—no mean feat—and they followed instructions to the letter but nothing happened. The next attempt at delivery is to be late this morning, but in the meantime—" He stopped.

"In the meantime what?"

Bishop grinned. "I'm only trying to milk the one slice of drama on a dull Friday, but in the meantime a video's been found in a Manhattan post office, left on a counter yesterday, with Bidwell pleading for his life. They've decided to air it publicly today on the twelve o'clock news."

"Bidwell, himself? Not his wife?"

Bishop nodded. "Bidwell himself, speaking from captivity. Incidentally, Jed says his wife is still under a doctor's care but one of the chaps at the house is of the opinion that it wouldn't matter all that much to Mrs. Bidwell if the abductors *did* kill her husband. Portrait of a happy marriage, what?"

"Only one amateur's opinion," Carstairs reminded him.

"Right, only one man's opinion," Bishop agreed with a smile.

Carstairs pointed to the small television set in the corner. "I'd like to hear that, I'll be interested in how Bidwell's been enduring his captivity. The noon news, you said? Remind me."

"You bet," said Bishop, and went back to his desk where at ten o'clock he made his sixth attempt to reach Willie and his Traveling Show in Maine, and again connected with his answering machine. "Foxy so-and-so," murmured Bishop, "I'll wager he's switched off his phone completely so he can sleep." He made a note to try again in an hour or so, and seeing the day's newspaper tucked in his IN basket he scanned the headlines, then turned to the second page for a quick glance. At the bottom of the page he found a small headline: RENEWED VIOLENCE IN UBANGIBA.

Carstairs's Ubangiba, he thought, and picking up a pair of scissors he cut it out for his attention, half humorously because of the strange interest Carstairs had been developing in the country these past few days. Before putting it aside he noted the words *rioting* and *two deaths*, and the fact that the Ubangiban *gwar*, once worth seventy-five cents to the U.S. dollar, was now worth only eight cents.

Poor Ubangiba, he thought.

Carstairs, in his office next door, had just completed the signing of three reports when a call came through from Allan in the Africa section.

"About Ubangiba," he reminded Carstairs. "The soil analysis has been done for you posthaste, and we'll be faxing the report to you in a few minutes."

Carstairs said, "Fine, but can you tell me now, briefly, the conclusion? Did they find possibilities?"

"Only one," said Allan. "There's a mountain running along the southern section of Ubangiba, not high—a line of hills, actually—and from his analysis, which you can struggle with once the report reaches you, the only possibility would be coal."

"Coal!" exclaimed Carstairs. "In Africa?"

"Yes, our geologist points out that by mid-century Algeria was operating four or five mines they'd found in the Sahara desert. At Kenadsa to the west of

Columb Bechar there was a vein of coal that produced 350,000 tons a year, for instance. Not pit mines, the seam runs through the hills in what he calls 'galleries.' About forty miles farther south they discovered a seam of coal of even better quality, and coal was later found at Ksi, Ksou, and Mazarif. If there's coal in Ubangiba it could be a remnant of the same primeval forest or marsh that ran through the area aeons ago. He doubts these mines are still in operation. They've probably closed down since the discovery of natural gas in the north, but coal there is, or was."

"Not much anyone can do with coal in the middle of nowhere," growled Carstairs. "No way to export it in a landlocked country, and the yield sounds damn small."

"Oh, I don't know," said Allan. "I would think in a country with no natural source of power except the sun it could do *something*. Heat and light a city or two, dig artesian wells, not to mention run a railroad or a few factories."

"Hmmm," murmured Carstairs. "Well, send the report along."

Coal, he thought as he hung up, and he admitted to disappointment. Oil and natural gas had pretty much supplanted coal, and coal scarcely seemed worth those concealed trips to Ubangiba to capture its mineral rights. What had Desforges said? Something to the effect that with cheap labor it could be modestly profitable. He'd said something else that Carstairs couldn't recall, something to do with cheap labor that nagged at his memory for a moment but without result; fortunately he had his conversation with Desforges on tape, when he had time to review it. For now, however, he could only feel baffled, and—he had to admit—a sense of let-down. He couldn't imagine a modest profit exciting a man like Bidwell with his ability to amass millions . . . or billions, according to Bishop.

He glanced at the news clipping that Bishop had left on his desk about the country, crumpled it up, and tossed it away. *I'm losing interest in this—thank God,* he thought, *and it was never my business, anyway.*

At half-past ten Bishop picked up his phone to once again dial Willie's 207 number. This time the phone was answered on its seventh ring.

"Sorry old chap," he told Willie, "but I'm tired of leaving my cheery voice on your machine, it's time I talk with Pete's cargo the other night, no matter how busy you are."

"It's time, yes," agreed Willie. "Incidentally, we'll be here at least one more night, the police insist on it. It will cost."

"Our problem, not yours," Bishop assured him. "We don't appreciate our people getting stabbed in the back."

"Right. Hold on, I'll fetch her."

A door opened and closed, and Bishop waited; presently faint voices were heard and at last that of Mrs. Pollifax, somewhat breathless. "Hello, I'm here," she said.

Bishop grinned. "So I notice, and it's been damn hard finding the right time to reach you. Carstairs, not to mention yours truly, wants to know what the devil happened to you two nights ago."

She said warmly, "And I want to thank you for rescuing us, Bishop."

"Yes, but from what?" he asked. "And who was chasing you, and who is the 'us'? Talk, for pete's sake."

He heard her take a deep breath. "Give me a minute to put it all together or it'll take hours." After a brief hesitation: "All right, it started with Kadi Hopkirk," she began, "who needed help and is here with me: age nineteen, grew up in Africa, now studying art in New York. She was interviewing for a job in New Haven when she ran into a boy she'd grown up with, a student now at Yale. They met on the street. This childhood friend of hers introduced the young man with him as his roommate, and then over coffee slipped her a note saying, *'Not roommate—guard.'* "

"I'm listening," Bishop told her.

"She left puzzled and rather alarmed. A van parked outside the coffee shop began following her—to the bus station—and then followed her bus down the turnpike. At some point after Bridgeport, in a panic, she asked the bus driver to stop, jumped out, and ran through a neighborhood of houses and gardens, unfortunately pursued by the two men on foot, and ended up hiding in my house for two days without Cyrus and me knowing it. And I might add," she said, "that during those two days the same van drove past my house often enough for me to notice it even before I found her hiding in a closet."

"Same one?" asked Bishop skeptically. "How could you tell?"

She said tartly, "No one could *help* but notice it was the van she described, because of the crazy sign on its panel, Chigi Scap Metal."

"You mean Chigi *Scrap* Metal, don't you?"

"No, scap—they'd left out the *r. Not* scrap."

"Okay, scap," he murmured. "And this girl. You found her in your house, but what sort is she? Believable?"

"A quite delightful missionary's child," said Mrs. Pollifax, "and as to believable I can testify to the fact that my house was entered and searched, after which we were followed up and down the Connecticut Turnpike for hours. We lost them in Worcester just long enough to register at a motel, but they found us there an hour later. My car's still there, we got away by taxi—to the hospital, where I called you."

Bishop was silent for a moment, puzzled by what he'd heard. He said at last, "Well, we can do something about your car, anyway. What motel? I'll send Pete for it."

"Bide-A-Wee," she told him. "It's near the highway exit, or in that area. But I'm very curious about Kadi's friend Sammy and I know she's worried about him."

"All very strange," admitted Bishop. "One wonders—but I've got this on tape for Carstairs, he'll want to get back to you—he's at a meeting Upstairs just now. Any progress on you-know-what?"

"No, but the police are here questioning everyone," she told him. "And so am I." She added brightly, "It was Willie's idea that I be a feature writer for a newspaper, I'm about to interview the Snake Woman."

"Snake Woman," repeated Bishop blankly. "Yes, of *course*, the Snake Woman."

"And Kadi is being sawed in half," she added blithely, and hung up.

Bishop grinned. He decided that Mrs. Pollifax was thoroughly enjoying herself in spite of those earlier protests about being "stuck" that Willie had described.

An hour later when Carstairs returned from his conference Upstairs Bishop told him, "I've finally connected with Mrs. Pollifax at Willie's; I've got it all on tape."

Carstairs nodded absently. "Good," he said in that voice that meant his thoughts were elsewhere.

"I *said*—" began Bishop again.

"Yes yes, I heard you," Carstairs said impatiently. "They've been able to question Lazlo at last, he's been patched up enough for an interview."

"Does he know who attacked him at Willie's?"

Carstairs looked at him blankly. "At the carnival? No, I wanted him questioned in more detail about what sent him to Willie's in the first place, on March 10th. They just faxed the results to Mornajay."

Thoroughly puzzled, Bishop said, "But so long ago. That's important?"

Carstairs glanced down at the sheaf of notes he carried. "We think he might have been followed from Boston to the carnival, which at least would prevent our closing down Willie as a safe house, and could possibly give us a clue as to who stabbed him a month later. Lazlo had been given a surveillance job in Boston, where he tailed a man named Kopcha into a tenement building. There he overheard scraps of conversation about a ransom pick-up in April."

Bishop whistled faintly. "A ransom pick-up in *April*?"

Carstairs nodded. "When Lazlo came out of that building he'd been beaten up and his arm was broken. That's when he went to Willie's."

"Bidwell was kidnapped in April, do you think possibly—?"

"I think *possibly*, yes," said Carstairs, but added sternly, "*Only* a possibility, however. If by chance it was Bidwell's abduction they were discussing, that tenement building could be where they planned to hold Bidwell, and where he may be hidden away now. I'd wanted more, but I'm not sure I have more."

Carstairs frowned, scanning the faxed sheets. "He'd already described the size of the building: it was tall, vacant, brick, most of its windows boarded up. . . . Asked to describe any possible identifying details on the street he remembered a fire hydrant at the vacant lot next to the building—not much help—

and a van parked in front of the tenement, rather grubby, he says, with a sign on it 'Chigi Scap Metal—' " His frown deepened. "A type error here, they must mean Chigi Scrap Metal—"

Bishop leaped out of his chair in excitement. "No, no, let me look!"

"What on earth," protested Carstairs. "All I said was . . ."

"I know, I know, you said, 'Chigi *SCAP* Metal'—and so did Mrs. Pollifax, it's on her tape, I tell you it's on her tape, she described just such a van and I said just what you said, 'You mean scrap, don't you?' and she said, 'No, Chigi SCAP Metal, they'd left out the *r*.' "

"Are you mad? How can Mrs. Pollifax—" Carstairs stopped and stared at Bishop in astonishment. "It has to be a mistake, what possible connection—" With an effort he rallied, to say quietly, "I think you'd better give me that tape, Bishop, and no calls for the next half an hour."

Carstairs retired to his office, and when he had listened to the tape of Mrs. Pollifax's conversation with Bishop he sat for a long time considering what he had heard. With a sudden glance at his watch he picked up the phone and prayed that Willie was in his trailer.

A woman's voice answered. Carstairs said, "Emergency call to Willie, his Uncle speaking."

The voice said, "This is Gertie. Just a minute, I see him talking outside the trailer."

Carstairs waited, but impatiently, and once connected he said, "Willie, this girl who arrived with Pete the other night. You know her at all? Name of Kadi?"

Willie said, "Nice kid, really knows how to handle a B-B gun."

"She's from Africa?"

"Yep."

"Happen to know what country, Willie?"

"Yep."

"So?"

"Ubangiba."

Carstairs felt a flick of excitement. He said quietly, "Thanks, Willie," and rang off to sit and scowl at his desk as if he could find an answer there. *Ubangiba again,* he thought . . . an abduction . . . a stabbing . . . a man in Boston who spoke of a ransom pick-up in April . . . Lecler and Romanovitch . . . a safe house, and a girl pursued by a Chigi Scap Metal van . . . and Desforges's report.

What *had* Desforges said that he wished he could recall? He picked Desforges's tape out of the rack and inserted it into his machine and listened with concentration to every word. He had said, "with cheap labor, and it would have to be *very* cheap labor—a bit Leopoldish, of course—but with cheap labor profitable, yes."

"Leopoldish" was the word he'd sought.

Carstairs reached for his dictionary and turned to Biographical Names. There were several Leopolds listed but if he understood Desforges correctly he had been referring to Leopold II, King of Belgium from 1865 to 1909.

Leopold and the Congo.

Carstairs replaced the dictionary and frowned; it was like a jigsaw puzzle, he thought, for which he held in his hand only a few pieces, none of them fitting yet and most of them missing, but there began to be a single intelligible thread. He sat for a long time over his puzzle, dropping one piece into place only to remove it and try another. At last he ran Desforges's tape again through the machine, and when the tape ended he said aloud to himself, "I have to be mad to think what I'm thinking—utterly mad—and yet I'm thinking it."

But it would certainly explain the huge ransom demanded for Bidwell's release.

He had reached one decision, however: in the morning, Saturday, he would send Bishop personally to Willie's in Maine. It was time to interview Kadi Hopkirk.

CHAPTER 14

MRS. POLLIFAX, ON HER WAY TO VISIT the Snake Woman, saw Boozy Tim slumped on a wooden crate next to the transformer. "Hello, Boozy Tim," she called out to him but he only mumbled a greeting and returned to scowling at the ground; without a smile on his face he looked shrunken and tired, all radiance gone.

Meeting Shannon in the trailer compound she asked, "What's wrong with Boozy Tim? He looks as if he's lost his last friend, he scarcely spoke to me."

"Off his feed," Shannon said, nodding. "One of those viruses, for sure. Sat next to him at breakfast, he stared at his food and left without touching it."

"What do you do here for a doctor?" asked Mrs. Pollifax.

Shannon chuckled. "I guess go see the girl who came with you, she's been telling me all about how medicine men cure things in Africa."

"Kadi has?"

Shannon grinned. "Yeah, her doctor-father was real interested, he knew a couple of them. Honey, would you believe that once, when a guy had gone crazy over there, some medicine man buried him alive in a pit for an hour—with a *goat*—then said a lot of incantations and when they dug him up the goat was dead and the madman alive? Cured, too, because her father checked him out."

"Sounds a reasonable equivalent of shock treatment," said Mrs. Pollifax, "but I doubt its use for Boozy Tim just now."

Shannon giggled. "No, we don't have a goat or a medicine man." With a glance at the sky, she frowned. "Don't like the look of those clouds."

"Rain?"

"A wipe-out night it if rains, honey. Where you off to now?"

Displaying her notebook and pen Mrs. Pollifax confided that she was on her way to the Snake Woman's long sleek trailer. "To interview her," she said, and aware that she was even more interested now in the man who lived with her, she added, "*And* her companion."

"Oh, Jock." Shannon made a face. "Funny. I know his type and believe me, his sort usually has an eye for the girls but he's too busy managing *her*." With a shrug she added, "Maybe that's why she lets him call the shots, to hold onto him, but he can sure be nasty. So good luck, honey."

It was Jock who opened the door to Mrs. Pollifax: lean, handsome, impatient, his eyes cold until he registered the fact that she was the woman from a newspaper, at which point he smiled, flashing perfect white teeth against his tanned skin. "Hey, Elda," he shouted. "Publicity. The interview lady." With exquisite politeness Mrs. Pollifax was ushered inside. "Have a seat—no, not that one, take this."

The Snake Woman walked out of an inner room saying doubtfully, "Publicity?"

Mrs. Pollifax scarcely recognized her this morning: there was no slash of scarlet across her lips, the curls had been sleeked back, and she wore a pair of horn-rimmed glasses. "Oh dear," she said, "I was feeding Herman."

"I'll do it," her companion told her, "but take off your glasses, will you?"

"You know I can't see much without them."

"Take them *off*," he said. "You want your picture in the papers with them?"

Mrs. Pollifax politely intruded to say, "No camera yet, that comes later."

At this Jock gave her an indignant glance but rallied to say, "Well, tell her how you grew up in Borneo, Elda." He walked out, presumably to feed Herman.

The Snake Woman smiled faintly. "I wasn't born in Borneo, of course, I grew up in farm country out

West, Nebraska, and then Montana. Would you like coffee?"

Mrs. Pollifax had seen enough of her surroundings by now to refuse, once her gaze had fallen upon the large glass cages that lined one wall of the room, each one occupied by what had looked like giant coils of rope until one of the ropes had drowsily stirred. Nor was she unaware of the white mouse that suddenly scampered across the room. Bringing out her notepad she said, "I see you really live with your snakes . . . let's begin with your name."

The Snake Woman sat down at the other end of the coffee table and said, "Okay, I'm Elda Higgins."

"And Jock, he's Higgins, too?"

"Oh no, we're not married. Not yet anyway," she said comfortably. "He's the one who talked me into this. I was teaching, you see, at a small midwestern college—teaching herpetology." Her voice sharpened, for a second became almost sarcastic as she added, "He told me what a lot of fun it would be, and lots of money, too, if I showed off my snakes at big expositions, seeing I had so many as pets." She rose and went to one of the cages and Mrs. Pollifax winced as she drew out a six-foot-long snake with brown stripes. "He likes to be held," she said, carrying him back to the chair. "He's a boa, isn't he beautiful? His name is Jimmy."

"Boa *constrictor*?" Mrs. Pollifax said weakly.

"Yes."

Recovering, Mrs. Pollifax asked if she was finding her new career fun and profitable.

Elda sighed. "Profitable? Well, it should be, it's just—" She hesitated. "No, not yet. We started the season with a big exposition in New York State and it looked great, but then Jock quarreled with the management, so we came here. We came late." She said with a wry smile, "So I can't say there's much money yet, no, this being so small a carnival."

Mrs. Pollifax smiled sympathetically. "I couldn't help but overhear yesterday—I was about to knock on your door—that you'd wanted to leave earlier."

Startled, Elda said, "Oh, Jock—Jock doesn't like the police." Aware that she'd been indiscreet she added quickly, "Really it was me, it just seemed as if we could do better somewhere else, it's not *that* late in the season. It's the money, you see, it costs to keep the place warm enough—nearly eighty degrees—for the snakes, and feeding them's expensive, and there's the travel, and the trailer payments, and I've got a daughter back in Nebraska . . ." Her voice trailed away as if she might cry if she continued.

"I'll write that down, it's very interesting," said Mrs. Pollifax, scribbling a few lines. "Have you known Jock long?"

"No, not long," she said and then, brightening, "but he knows carnivals and that sort of thing, he used to be a barker in the Strates Shows, and—"

"And sold you on the idea," said Mrs. Pollifax. "And the snakes, are they still highly dangerous?"

"No, not now," Elda said with a flash of anger.

"Not poisonous?"

The anger faded and she said without expression,

"Jock refused to live with me unless their venom ducts were cut." She gave an abrupt laugh that sounded false. "Well, he probably was right, because they don't like him, but I'll tell you this." She leaned forward, with passion in her voice, "No rattlesnake or any other snake ever, *ever*, bit me, I've raised them since I was a kid of seven or eight years old, and never, *never* did they hurt me."

"How do you do it?" asked Mrs. Pollifax, marveling.

Elda leaned back, relaxed again, to say easily, "Well, they *know* me, you see, we're friends. I talk to them, pet them, feed them, tame them. There aren't many deaths in the United States from snakes, you know, it's mostly from the diamond-back rattlers, and I don't fool with them. King snakes, boas, pythons, and sidewinders are what I have. *Three* gorgeous pythons." She nodded toward the cages along the wall. "Want to see them?"

"Uh—not just now. Would you call yourself a snake-charmer?"

Elda laughed. "Oh, there aren't any snake-charmers, just strong-minded people."

Strong-minded Elda might be, thought Mrs. Pollifax, but not where Jock was concerned. With an uneasy glance at the boa that was slithering out of Elda's lap she rose, saying, "I think this gives me enough material for the moment, I want to talk to some of the concessionaires I've not spoken with yet."

"Oh, them." Casually picking the boa up from the

floor, Elda opened the door for Mrs. Pollifax and blinked at the sun outside.

Mrs. Pollifax said, "Do you know any of your neighbors? Mingle at all?"

Elda said eagerly, "Oh I'd love—" She stopped and glanced back toward the kitchen. "No," she said. "No, I don't know any of them."

Jock again, thought Mrs. Pollifax, and left, feeling that she was not going to be of any help to Willie; any talents she might possess for ferreting out skullduggery had become sidetracked by the novelty of her surroundings. Considering Elda the Snake Woman, for instance, she thought her as caged as any of her pythons but this could, of course, be only a cover; she might instead be a consummate actress and not a professor of herpetology at all. The police had certainly made her companion Jock nervous but it was quite possible this was for reasons other than international espionage. . . . She had overheard the police interviewing Jasna and her father yesterday, and if his blindness was what had reduced them to bringing a class act to Willie's small carnival she thought they concealed his blindness very well. At the Ten-in-One last night she had witnessed their performance with much interest. In his white satin robe and with his full black beard he had resembled a Russian patriarch, the dark glasses quite understandable due to the brilliance of the spotlight trained on him. She noted that he had already been placed in position before the curtain was raised: the two worked hard at concealing his handicap. There was also Lubo, stubbornly and relentlessly secretive—even Kadi hadn't been able to pry any information from him—yet carnies, she realized, were not the usual run of people; in any normal society she supposed they would be called misfits: voluptuous Shannon, for instance, who scorned Broadway to move, move, move . . . Boozy Tim whose eccentricities were regarded here with pride and even awe; where else would he find so amiable and responsive an audience?

The sun had emerged again from behind the clouds, and its heat flavored the air with the scent of sawdust. She decided to see if Pie-Eye had opened up his Cat-Rack booth yet, and headed for the midway. The man called Jake was fussing with the transformer and gave her a nod as she passed. She had not yet met Pie-Eye but she had glimpsed him at his stall the night before and had noted the bright pink turban he wore around his head, setting off a lean and swarthy face with a pencil-line mustache that punctuated thin lips. Now she saw that his booth was open and that he was talking to—of all people—Kadi, which she thought would definitely make her questions easier. She strolled across the midway to join them.

"He's not pie-eyed," Kadi told her, "but nobody can pronounce his name so he's called that, but he doesn't like it. His name's really—" She looked at him questioningly.

"Pyrrhus," he announced. "The name of a king," he reminded her firmly.

"Yes indeed, and how do you do," said Mrs. Pollifax. "And you run the Cat-Rack game?"

He shrugged. "This year, this season, yes." He smiled at her benevolently.

"And other seasons?" she asked, returning his smile.

Again he shrugged. "Anything, everything! Mental telepathy, fortune-telling, Spin the Wheel, the penny-pitching board, I can do anything. I am a psychic and also," he admitted charmingly, "a genius."

"That's a great deal of talent," she told him, and added mischievously, "I wonder that you're here and not at one of the big expositions."

His charm at once vanished. He stared at her with suspicion, saying coldly, "I go where I choose—where my destiny points—I move with the wind."

"It's a southeast wind today," Kadi said ingenuously. "A hot one, too." She winked at Mrs. Pollifax and turned to leave. "Let's go find Boozy Tim, Emmy." Once out of hearing she whispered, "Nobody likes Pie-Eye, Gertie says they think he's a bit light-fingered and on the lam. Maybe he's the one."

"I'll make a note of that—and of your expanding vocabulary," teased Mrs. Pollifax. "Any more sketching?"

Kadi glanced down at her sketchbook. "Only of the two men in the Chigi Scap Metal van who chased me. At least I tried, except of course I never saw them close-up."

Glancing at the two faces Mrs. Pollifax murmured, "Older than I thought. Asian, perhaps? Rough and tough as well, from the look of them, not at all the sort anyone would appreciate being pursued by."

"No," said Kadi. "I just thought, if I tried to get them on paper, I might get them out of my dreams. They chased me into your garden last night, too, when I was asleep." Having stated this in a matter-of-fact voice she added with a smile, "Did you know Boozy Tim's sailed all around the world on cargo ships? Except that when Willie found him he was homeless and living on the streets."

"I didn't know that."

Kadi nodded. "There's more news I haven't told you: I've been offered three jobs already—three! Pogo, the Professor, and—don't faint—Willie. For the summer."

"Willie!"

Kadi nodded happily. "He wants me to make a sketch of him for his livingroom—although *not* to replace Elvis Presley—and to design new carnival posters and touch up the Ten-in-One canvases, especially El Flamo and the Dancing Girls."

Amused, Mrs. Pollifax said, "And have you said yes?"

Kadi looked troubled. "I told Willie I had to find out first about Sammy." Glancing up and down the midway she added, "Where can Boozy Tim be? Jake," she called to the ride foreman, "have you seen Boozy Tim?"

Jake gave her a shy smile; everyone smiled at Kadi, noticed Mrs. Pollifax; it was impossible not to, for she was blossoming like a girl at her first prom, her eyes shining, cheeks pink, dark hair blown into tangles.

"Boozy Tim?" repeated Jake. "Gone into town. Walked."

Surprised, Mrs. Pollifax said, "On such a hot day? Shannon said he wasn't feeling well this morning."

Jake frowned. "She offered him a ride but he said he wanted to walk." He shook his head. "Hardly ever leaves the show, guess he needed something really bad." He added consolingly, "He'll be okay, it's only three miles and Shannon said she'd keep an eye out for him to give him a ride back."

Mrs. Pollifax was considerably relieved to hear this.

She and Kadi approached their trailer together and Mrs. Pollifax unlocked the door, an act that proved more difficult than usual. "Stubborn," she said, inserting the key a second time and frowning.

"Maybe needs oiling," said Kadi.

"Certainly needs *something*." Once again Mrs. Pollifax withdrew and inserted the key in the lock and this time it turned hard but unlocked the door.

They walked in and Mrs. Pollifax said, "Oh-oh."

"What?" asked Kadi.

"You'd better find Willie, we've been searched," she told her. "Carelessly, too. I left my purse under the pillow, totally concealed, but now half of it's visible, and where's your knapsack?"

Startled, Kadi glanced quickly around the small

trailer. "It's on the seat by the table but I know I left it on my bunk. Emmy—"

"Find Willie, you can see if anything's missing when you get back. The side window's open and the screen knocked out. Whoever it was must have left in a hurry when they heard us outside."

With Kadi gone Mrs. Pollifax looked through her purse, finding its contents disarranged but nothing missing, not even the seventy dollars in her wallet. Whoever had searched it, however, would know now, from her checkbook and credit card, that her name was not plain Emmy Reed. She wondered how important this was.

When Willie at last arrived he looked grim. "Someone checking you out I do not *like*. What's missing?"

"I don't like it either," she responded, "and nothing at all has been stolen."

"Worse yet," said Willie, looking grimmer.

Kadi was groping through her knapsack, finally spilling its contents across the bunk: two chocolate bars, four sketchbooks, a change purse, wallet, a book, pens and pencils, a passport, three lipsticks, a brush and comb, and a small folder neatly lettered: *Résumé, Kadi Hopkirk.*

Mrs. Pollifax smiled a little at the collection. "All there?"

Kadi nodded.

"I don't like this at all," repeated Willie. "In broad daylight, too, and nothing missing. It makes me think whoever knifed Lazlo really *must* be here still and is getting nervous. Or curious. If you'd been robbed it would have been one thing, but with nothing taken—"

"Do you think my so-called interviews are making someone edgy?"

Willie considered this. "No," he said thoughtfully, "it's more likely someone feels watched."

"Certainly not by me," she said indignantly. "The only person I've consistently watched is the Professor, when he saws Kadi in half." Glancing past Willie to the window she saw Boozy Tim trudging past the trailer with a large white paper bag in one hand, and she gave a sigh of relief. "Thank heaven! There's Boozy Tim at last, we've been worried about him."

Willie looked grim again. "Just the person I want to see." Striding to the open door he called out to him, and stepped down from the trailer. The two met just outside the window. "Boozy Tim, what the hell's wrong with you, you been sick?" he demanded. "Everybody comes to me and wants to know what the hell's wrong with you today."

Boozy Tim said earnestly, "Just trying to *think*, Willie. Honest, Willie, if I could think *hard* enough I just know I could help with that Santa Claus fellow that stepped on my foot."

Willie's voice turned gentle. "Not sick, then?"

"No, Willie, just trying hard to *think*."

"Well, don't try anymore, Boozy Tim—*don't*," Willie told him. "We're all missing your smiles."

"You are, Willie? Really? Okay, Willie, I'll stop if you say so."

"I do say so. C'mon, let's hit Mick for a cup of coffee at the grab-joint, you look tired."

So that's it, thought Mrs. Pollifax; Boozy Tim had wanted desperately to please Willie, and it was no wonder if he had lived on the streets before being embraced by the carnies. Shannon had described the carnival as a family, and for the regulars who joined the show every year she could see that it must be exactly that.

Kadi, re-packing her knapsack, said, "Guess I'll take a shower now, it'll be show-time soon enough."

Mrs. Pollifax nodded. The incident had ended, she would presently restore the window screen to its frame, join the crowd for an early dinner at the cookhouse and at six the carnival would open, but she knew that it would not be quite the same, for something had changed: Lazlo's attacker was no longer a mysterious possibility but was becoming a presence.

At six o'clock Mrs. Pollifax moved against the influx of townies streaming through the gate to head for the Ten-in-One. She walked to the sound of the merry-go-round playing the lilting strains of the "Blue Danube," and by the time she entered the big tent the music had changed to a jolly "Ciribiribin." It seemed like ritual now to watch Kadi's first performance of the evening and then accompany Kadi as she hurried over to Pogo's shooting gallery to become his stick for fifteen or twenty minutes. Once inside the tent she paused beside the Talking Sphinx—*Ask Any Question, the Sphinx Will Answer You!*—and wished she could ask if it was Lazlo's attacker who had searched their trailer this afternoon, but the young ventriloquist behind the sphinx would only think her quite mad.

It was a warm night, even warmer under the Ten-in-One canvas. She took her place in the bleachers and watched Norbert the Contortionist wrap his legs around his neck, marveled at El Flamo the Fire-eater; and then as the Professor arrived on the stage she turned her head to see what sort of business the carnival was pulling in this night. It was now that she saw Boozy Tim standing in the shadow of the bleachers watching, his eyes narrowed and as intent as laser beams. He had said, *Honest, Willie, if I could think hard enough I just know I could help with that Santa Claus fellow,* and Willie had said, *Don't try anymore, Boozy Tim, don't.*

Obviously Boozy Tim was still trying; he was studying every move the Snake Woman made, his face clouded and somber. The Snake Woman retired and the Professor appeared on stage, and Boozy Tim watched him closely, too. After the Professor, thought Mrs. Pollifax, there would come Jasna and her father, and then El Flamo the Fire-eater, and she began to admit a feeling of deep uneasiness. *He shouldn't, he really shouldn't,* she thought, because in his attempt to identify the person who had stepped on his foot two nights ago he would soon become conspicuous; and with a shock she recalled Willie saying, "It's more likely someone feels watched."

She wanted to say to him, "Stop watching like that, it's dangerous," but her decision was distracted by the ending of the Professor's act and Kadi appearing at her side. Nevertheless as they passed Boozy Tim, Mrs. Pollifax stopped. "Boozy Tim," she said in a low voice, "come outside with us, won't you? Kadi and I are off to Pogo's and you can keep me company. Do come!"

"Yes'm," he said politely, not removing his eyes from the stage. "In a little while. Not yet."

He was still watching as they left the Ten-in-One.

CHAPTER 15

BISHOP DID NOT RECEIVE KINDLY THE news that on Saturday morning he was to fly to Maine and interview Kadi Hopkirk. "Damn it," he protested, "I've a date tomorrow to lunch and play golf, I've only just met this blonde, she's stunning, and she *likes* me."

"I like you, too," said Carstairs dryly. "So does Mrs. Pollifax. Even Kadi Hopkirk may like you."

Bishop sniffed indignantly. "I might point out that none of you are blonde, with sylphlike figures, work for the Treasury Department, and can talk in depth about the Federal Reserve."

Carstairs raised an eyebrow. "Talk about the Federal Reserve? Oh, please, Bishop."

"Oh well." Bishop grinned sheepishly. "If I've expressed my disappointment clearly enough I'll stop, but there are times—"

"What we're paid for," Carstairs reminded him. "However, you'll be at Willie's by two in the afternoon and should be back by evening, I promise you a free Sunday, and you're the only person I trust for the job."

Having admitted this he returned to his usual brisk self. "Now I want two things done: I want inquiries sent out to the state police in New York, Connecticut, and New Jersey regarding a white van with the name Chigi Scap Metal on its panels, license unknown. Mrs. Pollifax didn't happen to notice the *color* of the plate, did she?"

Bishop shook his head. "It could very well have been neatly muddied and obscured for daytime, and unlit for night driving, but since it was always behind them it's not too surprising if they didn't notice." He glanced at his watch. "I'll get to work on the police calls, but what was that second job?"

Carstairs smiled. "Whenever it feels right for you—at the proper time this afternoon—you might give Jed Addams a call at the FBI and learn whether this morning's ransom drop-off met with any success. Now let me get back to work, you know how Fridays are."

"On my way." At the door Bishop hesitated, turning to say with a grin, "I admit there are compensations in regard to the trip to Maine. When I spoke with Mrs. Pollifax she was about to happily interview a Snake Woman. I'll be interested in how she deals with a carnival, it should be quite a change from her Garden Club."

"Even more interesting if she's learning who knifed Lazlo," pointed out Carstairs, but Bishop had already closed the door behind him and didn't hear.

Promptly at 11:57 the television was turned on; a soap opera was just ending and Bishop watched a voluptuous blonde actress with enormous interest. After two commercials came the excited announcement that Henry Bidwell had at last been heard from, and was presumably still alive, and the film was flashed on the screen. It had been filmed by an amateur, the lighting was poor, the background blurred, but Bidwell's face was close to the camera and clear enough for a bruise on one cheek to be seen, and smudges under his eyes. His voice was tired. He said that he was Henry Bidwell, that he was not being ill-treated but the ransom had still not been paid, he had been told that the police had fouled up several attempts and he was begging them to expedite the payment because he was now in fear of his life. "I beg of you," he pleaded, "for God's sake return me to my family before they kill me, *these are not patient people.*"

Abruptly it ended.

"Dramatic," said Carstairs, nodding.

"Dramatic!" exploded Bishop. "Not ill-treated, but did you see the bruise on his cheek? The FBI had jolly well better stop fooling around or they'll have blood on their hands."

Carstairs gently pointed out that pick-ups were not so easily arranged.

Bishop sniffed. "Jed Addams said the last attempt was out on a country road in New Jersey, no doubt with an agent up every tree and a helicopter circling."

Amused, Carstairs said, "And just how would you plan delivery and pick-up, then?"

Bishop scowled. "Well, I'd—" He stopped. "A busy street corner in New York? Drop it maybe in a litter basket, one of those wire things?"

"You'd leave fifty million in unmarked bills in a litter basket on a street corner, and hope no vagabond would get to it first?"

Bishop said irritably, "Well, I don't know, but it's their job to come up with something creative, isn't it?"

"Yes," agreed Carstairs, "but not so creative they scare off the kidnappers who want to be certain they're not being watched, photographed, or followed." He glanced at the clock. "Now 12:07 . . . well, we've seen Bidwell. Don't get so bogged down in paperwork you forget to check with Jed Addams about the latest attempt."

"How could I forget? I thought about 2:30?"

"Sounds good."

Once alone Carstairs attacked his own paperwork, was called Upstairs for a conference with Mornajay and returned at three o'clock to find Bishop looking pleased. "It's finally happened," he said. "The ransom. I don't know how, but at first light—at 5 o'clock this morning—the Bidwell son proved useful after all.

He accomplished the delivery on a motorcycle or bicycle somewhere near the estate, and before he even reached home the kidnappers confirmed by a prearranged signal that the pick-up was successful. Now all they have to do is wait in suspense for Bidwell to be delivered safely, too."

"Not bad for a week's work," said Carstairs. "And somebody had a good head on his shoulders—not too light, not too dark at five A.M. Good show!"

At half-past five in the afternoon Carstairs was dictating notes to Bishop and finishing up the last work of the day when the buzzing of the phone interrupted them. "Carstairs here," he said and a minute later, placing his hand over the receiver, he told Bishop, "It's the New York police, they've found the Chigi Scap Metal van." He returned to the phone, said, "*Where?*" in a startled voice, and then, "Empty? And how long?" He made a face. "Right. I appreciate your help, we'll be in touch." He hung up, looking sober and a little sad, until Bishop forced himself to ask, "So where did they find the van?"

Carstairs sighed. "It's just been pulled out of the East River. Someone on the docks heard a big splash over an hour ago and saw the last of it go down and called the police."

Bishop whistled through his teeth. "Anyone in it?"

"One body. That of the driver, but they say the window and door on the passenger side were open so there may have been two of them. Poor devils, no matter what their crimes."

Bishop stared at him, appalled. "Does any of this make sense?"

"It could," said Carstairs noncommittally. "It might. It may." Turning his attention to Bishop he said, "It's getting late, you'd better go home and pack your bag, the helicopter will take you to Maine in the morning."

"Yes, but if anything else is going to happen—"

"Nothing else is going to happen," Carstairs told him, "I'll be leaving shortly, too."

With a wry smile Bishop said, "But not immediately? What's left to do?"

"Think," said Carstairs wearily.

"Oh," said Bishop, and went out.

When he had gone Carstairs switched off his phones to sit quietly at his desk and go over the same old puzzle again, updating it by rote: an abduction, a stabbing . . . a man in Boston who spoke of a ransom pick-up in April . . . Lecler and Romanovitch . . . Desforges's report . . . a girl from Ubangiba pursued by a Chigi Scap Metal van, and to this he could now add Bidwell's $50 million ransom paid and one Chigi Scap Metal van hauled out of New York's East River.

"Their usefulness over—they knew too much," he said aloud. "Very well thought out and engineered. Very!"

But there were still several pieces of the puzzle missing—important ones—and he frowned over these for a long time until he glanced at his watch, realized he was hungry, and decided that he might think better if he had some food.

In the table-service room he ordered a lamb chop, spinach, and a baked potato and tried to remember if he'd had any lunch. He doubted it, and congratulated himself on his decision to inject nourishment into his thought processes. He was trying to decide whether to order apple pie or ice cream for dessert when he saw Allan from the Africa section heading toward him, a lanky young man with a head of bright red hair whose last name he couldn't remember.

It was possible, he thought, that he'd never known it.

"Hi," Allan said. "I was just leaving and spotted you. Didn't realize you were still in the building or I'd have called you."

"Called me?"

Allan nodded amiably. "Yeah. Don't know whether it would interest you or not, but you did ask for that geological report on Ubangiba, right?"

"Yes indeed," said Carstairs.

"The news was on the BBC an hour ago that their President's dead."

Carstairs looked at him in surprise. "Are we talking about Ubangiba?"

"Right."

"And President-for-Life Simoko is dead?"

Allan nodded. "Just thought I'd tell you in case it's of any interest," he said, and with a smile and a nod he continued on his way toward the exit.

Carstairs sat very still, thinking how very much this did interest him, so much so that he forgot dessert and returned at once to his office to begin a series of phone calls, several of them to Europe, and one of them to Bishop.

CHAPTER 16

ON SATURDAYS THE LIFE OF THE CARNIval changed drastically because it was matinee day, the gates opened at two in the afternoon, the acts in the Ten-in-One were reversed—the last one seen first—and the take was the biggest of the week, barring rain. Whether there would be crowds today was a matter of speculation, since under normal circumstances the carnival would have left during the night to establish itself sixty miles to the north. Now it remained to be seen whether their attractions had been exhausted; over lunch in the cook-house there was still a fair amount of grumbling over no tear-down during the night, and their being trapped here for an additional day. A Saturday, too.

Any worry about the weather had dissipated: it was June-hot with a small breeze distributing the usual smells of the carnival: hot popcorn, grease, sawdust, and the freshly cut grass in the field beyond. As Mrs. Pollifax and Kadi left the grab-joint they were accosted by Willie with an odd expression on his face. "I don't get it," he told them, "I can't find Boozy Tim. Jake hasn't seen him, Shannon hasn't seen him today, nobody knows where he is. Do you? Have you seen him?"

Mrs. Pollifax stiffened. "You're sure he's not in his trailer?"

Willie shook his head. "It's locked up tight. I looked through the back window and nobody's inside. What's the matter?"

"What's the matter," said Mrs. Pollifax slowly, "is that last night in the Ten-in-One, waiting for Kadi, Boozy Tim was there studying each of the acts and watching *intently*, apparently still looking for the person who stepped on his foot. I tried to stop him, but—"

Willie, staring at her in astonishment, said, "You mean he kept at it, when damn it he promised me?" And then, assimilating the reality of it, "Where was he standing, was he conspicuous?"

"Anybody in the aisles is conspicuous from the stage," pointed out Mrs. Pollifax, "but at least when Kadi and I left he was pretty much in shadow. I don't know how obvious he became after that."

Willie said grimly, "And here I thought he was sleeping late because of his damnfool walk into town yesterday. He's frail, you know. I think we've got to call in the *gavver* on this."

"Gavver?"

"Police. They're still guarding the exits but there's one of them in my trailer now making a phone call, the sandy-haired one called Bix."

Kadi said earnestly, "I can help look, *everybody* can help, Willie. You think he had a heart attack or something?"

Mrs. Pollifax caught Willie's eye and held it. "Are you thinking what I'm thinking?"

His lips thinned. "You're damn right, but let's keep this quiet, we open in forty minutes. No panic. Wait here. No, come along with me."

"What is it?" asked Kadi, hurrying behind Willie with Mrs. Pollifax.

She said, "You remember my telling you what Boozy Tim saw on Wednesday night, the man with a white beard hurrying away from the crowd. He thought—felt—there was something familiar about him; now we're afraid Boozy Tim may have discovered who it was."

"You mean he's been trying to find—and maybe did?" gasped Kadi. "Oh God, if anything's happened to him!"

They were close behind Willie when he flung open the door to his trailer, and they followed him inside. The officer he'd called Bix was sitting at his desk, phone in hand. Willie said, "Trouble, Bix, Boozy Tim's missing. Nobody's seen him since last night."

Startled, Bix said, "The little guy, the one who saw—"

"Yeah." Willie was leaning over his desk and opening a drawer and Mrs. Pollifax's eyes widened as she saw him draw out a small, snub-nosed black gun, load it, and tuck it into his belt.

Bix returned to the phone to say, "Trouble, Chief, better call in a few state police. Got to hang up." At once he was on his feet. "Where do we look? Going to announce this over the loudspeaker?"

Willie shook his head. "The exits are still guarded, so he has to still be here. It's best we don't broadcast this, or whoever's fooling with Boozy Tim might—might—" He didn't finish, saying instead, "Let's you and me do the empty warehouse trucks—the trailers can wait until they're empty—and Emmy here, and Kadi, you check the booths. Under, over, and behind. Damn it, we open in thirty minutes and the place will be full of people—impossible!" Handing both Mrs. Pollifax and Kadi flashlights he added, "Let's meet in fifteen minutes at Boozy Tim's trailer."

They separated quickly, Mrs. Pollifax and Kadi heading out into the midway. Most of the booths were already open and at Lubo's their reception was hostile. "Why the hell should I let you prowl around my counter?" he demanded.

"Because Boozy Tim's missing," Mrs. Pollifax told him crossly.

"What—that nice little guy?"

"Just get out of our way and don't waste our time."

To Mrs. Pollifax's surprise he immediately stepped back and allowed them to open a coat locker in the rear and inspect every dark corner.

Up and down the midway the two of them went: the fortune teller's tent, Wheel of Fortune, the slum skillo joints, the Milk-bottle and Spindle games, the Bingo tent, Penny arcade, the merry-go-round, Whip, ferris wheel, and Dodge-'em cars. . . . There was no Boozy Tim, and their search consumed twenty minutes of precious time, so that it was only ten minutes before opening time when they rushed back to Boozy Tim's trailer to find that Willie and Bix were late, too.

Waiting outside, Mrs. Pollifax peered into Boozy Tim's trailer through the only window at her level and found her glance meeting an opposite wall inside, on which movie-star cut-outs occupied nearly every inch, running the gamut from Janet Gaynor to Madonna. She could see a tiny sink piled high with unwashed dishes, and a corner of his dining table on which lay the white paper bag that Boozy Tim had carried with him on his return from town yesterday. But there were other objects on the table as well, puzzling shapes she couldn't identify from this vantage point, and half of them cut off from view.

"You're frowning," said Kadi, "what is it? Is Boozy Tim there?"

"No, but I'm seeing the paper bag he brought from town yesterday, and something strange on the—go find Willie, Kadi—*fast*!"

"I see them on the midway talking to Jake."

"Then get them here quickly!" commanded Mrs. Pollifax.

After one look at Mrs. Pollifax's face Kadi raced toward the two men, shouting, and returned with them. "You didn't go inside earlier?" Mrs. Pollifax demanded of Willie. "I think it's terribly important."

"I'll get the skeleton key," said Willie.

"No—break down the door," she told him. *"Now."*

"Break down—but why?"

"I don't *know* why," she cried in frustration, "it's a *feeling* I have. *Please.*"

The door resisted, splintered and opened, and Mrs. Pollifax led them to Boozy Tim's dining table.

There was an open tin of white paint, a tin of talcum powder, a smear of ketchup, a paint brush, and two dark false beards, one of them half-painted white, the other one pure white with talcum dust surrounding it, as if the entire tin of talcum had been emptied over it.

This, thought Mrs. Pollifax, was what he'd walked into town to buy: Boozy Tim, deeply troubled, doubting himself, and afraid of what he suspected, had wanted to be sure.

Kadi, leaning over the small splash of red, said, "This isn't ketchup, it's blood."

They stared in shock at the splotch of red.

Willie said, "It must have happened last night, then, his trailer lighted, someone at the window seeing what he was experimenting with—"

"—and walked in on him," finished Bix.

"Oh dear God," whispered Kadi.

In a stunned voice Mrs. Pollifax said, "But there's only one person working in this carnival with a full beard."

"That's true," gasped Kadi. "It's true, she's right."

With a glance at his watch Willie said grimly, "It's 2:03 and we're open now. *And the acts are reversed in the afternoon shows.*"

They stared at one another in shock, and then Willie shouted, "RUN! And Bix—call in your police!"

It was proving a profitable afternoon for the Ten-in-One; the bleachers were full, the Snake Woman was just completing her act, and as the audience applauded and she left the stage Jasna took her place, strolling in casually, all silver in a sequined jumpsuit, very tall and very calm. With a curt bow to the audience she placed her case of knives on a tall stool, opened the case and displayed the knives that glittered in the spotlight. The audience settled into silence, watching intently. Selecting one of the knives she gestured toward the curtain, which slowly rose to reveal the backboard and her father standing against it, but in a strikingly different costume this afternoon: a long black robe and a hood that concealed half of his face.

Except the figure was smaller than Jasna's father, and did not stand up straight but sagged, head lowered until it rested on his chest, *and there was no beard.*

"It's Boozy Tim" gasped Mrs. Pollifax. "Willie—

Kadi—it's Boozy Tim up there, she's going to kill him and call it an accident!"

"Not in *my* carnival," said Willie grimly. Eyes narrowed, he said, "We've got about one minute, she won't dare kill him on the first throw, I'd guess the second or third, but we can't crowd her, if she sees us she'll kill him right away."

Mrs. Pollifax said desperately, "I know karate but I'd never be able to get near her, not close *enough*."

"And I'm wearing a gun," Willie said furiously, "but at that distance—I'm not that good."

"Give the gun to Kadi," she told him quickly. "Kadi, she doesn't know you . . . walk fast to the other side of the bleachers and pray you can shoot the knife out of her—" She faltered as Jasna aimed and threw the first knife, and the audience gasped as it pierced the backboard next to Boozy Tim's left shoulder. "—out of her hand. Hurry," she whispered as Willie handed her the small snub-nosed gun. Kadi tucked it into her belt and vanished behind the bleachers.

Slowly Mrs. Pollifax began to move down the aisle as if looking for a seat, her mind running over possible karate strikes, all of them impossible with Jasna on a stage several feet above the ground, and too far from the edge of the stage to be reached with a blow to an ankle. She was aware of Willie following behind her, doubled over so that he'd not be seen, and she fervently hoped this sudden activity in both of the aisles would not catch the eye of the woman on the stage.

Jasna reached for her second knife, aimed it, and sent it flying to a point an inch from Boozy Tim's right shoulder, where it hung, quivering; and now, picking up speed, she reached for the third knife, and—

A shot rang out. A woman screamed. The knife fell from Jasna's hand and for just a second she stood frozen, staring incredulously at the knife on the floor and then Mrs. Pollifax reached the stage, rushed across it, and thrust Jasna off-balance with a blow across her shoulders. As she staggered, Willie grabbed both of Jasna's arms and held them tightly behind her as the Ten-in-One was suddenly full of police in uniform rushing down the aisles.

Mrs. Pollifax hurried to the figure slumped against the backboard and pushed back the hood. "Hand me one of the knives," she shouted to Willie. "He's unconscious and tied here with a rope."

Willie thrust a struggling Jasna into the arms of a policeman, handed Mrs. Pollifax a knife, and turned to the audience. "Sorry, folks," he said, "a little trouble here but the show goes on." To someone behind the curtain he shouted, "For God's sake bring on Shannon and Zilka," and then he joined Mrs. Pollifax in sawing the thick rope that had kept Boozy Tim barely upright. Released, Tim fell into their arms and they carried him off the stage.

"Is he alive?" whispered Mrs. Pollifax as they laid him on the floor behind the curtain.

Kadi, rushing in to join them, gasped, "Is he alive? Will he be all right?"

"He still has a pulse but it's weak," said Willie, on his knees beside him. "Heavily drugged, I'd guess. Damn them anyway . . . Kadi, call an ambulance, the phone's in my office and—ah, there you are, Bix, we need an ambulance on the double. Did you find Jasna's father?"

"Did you think I would?" His voice was bitter. "I'll phone in his description as soon as I've called the ambulance, he can't have gotten far if he's blind." He stopped, looking shocked. "But he can't be blind."

"No, not blind," said Mrs. Pollifax. "Call the ambulance. Take Kadi with you, she's seen enough for one day."

"Right," said Bix. "Come on, Kadi, let's *go*."

When she hesitated Willie looked up and said, "And give her a shot of brandy, bottom drawer my desk."

As they hurried away Mrs. Pollifax whispered, "He looks—almost dead. Are you finding a heartbeat?"

"That too is faint," said Willie. "If you're into praying, pray."

"I feel more like crying," said Mrs. Pollifax shakily.

"Then you cry and I'll pray," Willie told her and they sat with Boozy Tim between them while on the other side of the curtain Shannon and Zilka performed their bumps and grinds to the music of "Toot Toot Tootsie."

* * *

Twenty minutes later Boozy Tim was carried out of the Ten-in-One on a stretcher, and with sirens screaming the ambulance made its exit, Pogo and Jake following in Shannon's car. A shaken Mrs. Pollifax and Willie left the scene to walk back to his trailer and wait for news from the hospital. Even among carnies the show had to go on, and an equally shaken Kadi had returned to the Ten-in-One to join the Professor and Tatiana and be sawed in half. Crossing the compound, Mrs. Pollifax found it utterly unreal to hear in daylight the beat of the merry-go-round music and the usual screams from the ferris wheel. She thought it unreal, too, when Willie said, "I guess we move on tonight if the police are satisfied. A busy night ahead!" Abruptly he came to a halt. "What the devil!"

Mrs. Pollifax jumped. "What? *What,* Willie?"

He pointed. "Helicopter landing in the field."

"Police?"

"No—no, it looks like Pete."

They stood beside Willie's trailer staring out at the field where the helicopter had come to a rest like a glittering insect in the bright sunlight; the hatch opened and two men jumped down, followed by Pete. The three men began walking toward them across the newly clipped field: Pete in a scarlet zip-up jacket; a stocky gray-haired man in a business suit; and a younger man with sandy hair and an agreeable face that Mrs. Pollifax recognized at once. "It's Bishop!" she exclaimed. "It's actually Bishop, but what can he possibly be doing here?"

A moment later, nearing them, Bishop called out a hello to Willie, and to Mrs. Pollifax, "I've come to take you and Kadi Hopkirk back to Carstairs. . . . No time to waste, you've fifteen minutes to collect your gear."

Mrs. Pollifax stared at him blankly: two worlds were suddenly in collision here on this sunny field, and Bishop's world had nothing to do with the merry-go-round music behind her, or with Boozy Tim, or with Jasna, or the tide of voices from the midway. She said indignantly, "I can't possibly leave now, Bishop, we've just learned who knifed Lazlo, the police have taken Jasna away but nobody's found her father yet, Boozy Tim's been drugged and taken to the hospital and they may have killed him, and—"

It was Bishop's turn to look blank. Pulling himself together he interrupted to say, "But Carstairs needs you. I brought Charlie to replace you but now he can stay and find out what the hell you're talking about. Right now Carstairs wants to know about Chigi Scap Metal."

"Chigi Scap Metal?" she faltered.

"Fifteen minutes," he reminded her.

After the events of this day even the Chigi Scap Metal van felt distant to her. With a sigh of exasperation Mrs. Pollifax turned back to the midway and made her way toward the Ten-in-One to find Kadi, thinking stormily that it was obvious neither Carstairs nor Bishop understood carnivals, or that by summoning Kadi they were depriving Pogo of his stick and the Professor of Tatiana's feet . . . and of herself, she admitted, and was furious.

CHAPTER 17

MRS. POLLIFAX WAS STILL NURSING A DIS-tinct feeling of anger when Bishop ushered her and Kadi into Carstairs's office. It was nearly seven o'clock but not even two and a half hours on a helicopter had diminished her indignation at being forcibly removed from Willie's. She was sure that absolutely nothing Carstairs had to say could make up for her being torn away from the carnival before she could learn whether Boozy Tim would survive, who Jasna was, and whether her father had been found yet.

After only one glance at her Carstairs said, "You're angry."

"Very," she snapped.

"And no doubt hungry, too," he added. "There are

trays on the way up from the cafeteria with dinner for the three of you . . . and you're Kadi Hopkirk," he said, smiling at her. "Are you angry, too?"

She grinned. "Mostly hungry. But very curious, of course, it's certainly been a strenuous few days."

He nodded. "Chigi Scap Metal."

Mrs. Pollifax forgot her anger to say, "But how did *you* hear about Chigi Scap Metal?"

"Obliquely," he told her. "It looks as if it or they may be linked to a case I've become interested in, and in which I've been pursuing a few tenuous leads. For instance, the men in the van may have been involved with whoever attacked Lazlo on Wednesday night at Willie's. A month ago the van was noted by Lazlo in Boston, parked outside a tenement house where he was also attacked, his arm broken, after possibly overhearing something of importance."

Mrs. Pollifax said eagerly, "Willie said Lazlo arrived at the carnival with a broken arm."

Carstairs nodded. "Yes, and we feel pretty sure the men he overheard in the tenement suspected that he'd heard too much and someone decided he was dangerous. Actually Lazlo had overheard very little but they didn't know that. Ah, but here comes your dinner. Bishop, bring in tray tables, will you, and then I want to hear about what I dragged you away from at Willie's this afternoon."

A bowl of hot chili was set before each of them, with corn muffins and butter, and a carafe of coffee for the three of them. Mrs. Pollifax, picking up a spoon, explained, "You have to understand first about Boozy Tim."

"I beg your pardon?"

"Boozy Tim was *nice*," Kadi said at once. "And he'd met God, you know."

Once this had been explained Mrs. Pollifax added, "He finally realized that the man who stepped on his foot after the 'Hey Rube'—the man with the Santa Claus beard—had to be Jasna's father. Perhaps the way he walked when he thought no one was watching—"

Kadi interrupted to say, "Except I wouldn't have put it past Boozy Tim to sneak under Jasna's trailer and listen, or peek in windows, and if once he guessed that Jasna's father couldn't be blind—"

"But his beard wasn't white," put in Mrs. Pollifax. "Once it was suggested to him that the man might have used a disguise, Boozy Tim walked into town, bought two false beards, and came back to experiment with what might change an authentic black beard for only an hour or so. Except unfortunately he confided in no one, and obviously the man was precisely the one we looked for. . . . We think Jasna and her father gagged him—there was blood on the table—and carried him back during the night to their trailer to decide what to do with him. He had to be killed, but it had to look like an accident, as if he'd taken the place of Jasna's father that night, and her aim—"

"Would have *killed* him," finished Kadi in an astonished voice, "Which I must say has left Jasna holding the bag once her father got away. Somehow . . . I drew a sketch of Jasna," she told Carstairs.

"Yes and she's extremely good," put in Mrs. Pollifax, "it might help to identify her."

"Help we can use," Carstairs told her. "Otherwise someone merely named Jasna—"

Kadi dug into her knapsack for her sketchpad and turned the pages to her sketch. "Here she is."

Carstairs studied the drawing and frowned. Handing it to his assistant he said, "Bishop, get the files on Olga Broniewski; the Broniewskis were in show business in Europe, and except for the butchered hair, damned if this doesn't look like her." As Bishop abandoned his chili to search the files, Carstairs added, "If that's who Jasna is, that bearded blind 'father' of hers would have been her husband Tamas."

"Husband?" echoed Mrs. Pollifax.

He nodded. "In his mid-thirties, and a ruthless chap—a dangerous pair, they usually travel with a circus." After a quick glance at the two photos that Bishop handed him he nodded. "Take a look."

Mrs. Pollifax looked, and sat back satisfied. "That's certainly Jasna, but with longer hair."

Kadi, staring at the photograph of the man, stammered, "B-but that's her blind father? He's young and incredibly handsome!"

Amused, Carstairs said, "A lesson for you in what disguise can do. It certainly explains how he got away. I'd guess that once he helped his wife dress and drug your Boozy Tim, and roped him to the backboard, he simply trimmed his beard and strolled through the gates when the carnival opened. A handsome young man returning to his car, or looking for his girlfriend . . ."

"But where's the connection?" asked Mrs. Pollifax.

Carstairs ignored this. "Any other sketches, Kadi?"

"I've a snapshot of Sammy," she told him, reaching into her knapsack and bringing out her wallet.

Carstairs reached out for the photo but his glance lingered a moment on Kadi's face, and Mrs. Pollifax decided that he didn't often see anyone so fresh and young in his office. Leaning over, Kadi pointed. "There's Sammy."

"Sammat, grandson of a King," murmured Carstairs. "Nice face."

"A *good* face," Kadi said firmly. "Can you, *will* you, help him?"

"Oh yes," he said.

Surprised, Mrs. Pollifax said, "It's important?"

"Very. Let me consider for a moment," said Carstairs, "because there's a great deal to do."

They sat and waited while he stared at the ceiling, glanced at Kadi, smiled vaguely at Mrs. Pollifax, and at last said crisply, "Kadi, I need the full name of your friend Sammy: how he would be registered at Yale."

"Sammat Yusufu."

"And his roommate's name?"

"He was introduced as Clarence Mulimo."

Carstairs wrote the names on a memo and said to Bishop, "Put through a call to the New Haven police department, will you, Bishop? Tell them I'll be there—" He glanced at his watch. "By nine o'clock at the latest, but first I want to speak to the chief on the phone."

"New Haven police?" gasped Kadi. "Oh, but please, that will—"

"Steady," counseled Carstairs. "I want two officers sent to the university to bring your Sammy to the police station for questioning about a stolen car."

"But Sammy would never, *never* steal a car," protested Kadi.

Carstairs smiled at her forgivingly. "He can explain that to the police at the station. It's the only way we can separate him from that roommate of his."

"Ah," murmured Mrs. Pollifax, intrigued by such beautiful deviousness.

"And you will be going with me to New Haven," Carstairs told them. "You, Mrs. Pollifax, and Kadi, too. Order a plane for us, Bishop, and after you've done that I want the passenger lists checked on every plane flying to Paris this weekend—names, Bishop, names. Who does wigs?"

"W-wigs?" stammered Bishop.

"Wigs."

"That would be Hazard's department."

"Good. Take Kadi with you and fit her out with a blonde wig, find some colorful touristy clothes for her, and above all a pair of dark glasses. Large ones. Mrs. Pollifax, I don't know what your plans may have been before this interruption in your life, or how much you care to tell that husband of yours, but I'm preempting you for a few days; you can use Helga's phone to call him. You and Kadi are accompanying me to Ubangiba."

"Ubangiba!" cried Kadi happily.

"Ubangiba?" repeated Mrs. Pollifax. "Accompanying you? *YOU* are going to Ubangiba?"

Bishop laughed. "You really are planning skullduggery—and going yourself?"

With a grin Carstairs said, "High time, Bishop . . . living behind a desk grows tiresome, and what I have in mind is going to need enormous tact, duplicity, diplomacy, and a great deal of bluffing, or the State Department will have my head. You'll take over for me, Bishop, I've cleared it with Mornajay." To the others he said, "Now carry those trays of food somewhere else—go away, out!—while I put in a call to the New Haven police, and to Paris. And while we're in New Haven, Bishop, have passports issued for Mrs. Pollifax and daughter Kadi—no, make it Katherine."

"Right, sir," said Bishop, added this to his list, and ushered Kadi and Mrs. Pollifax into his office, and Mrs. Pollifax into Helga's cubicle where she could call Cyrus.

The phone number of the hotel at which Cyrus was spending his last night was duly found, and she asked to speak with Cyrus Reed, present for the American Bar Association meetings. The desk clerk rang his room, and rang and rang. He said at last, "If he's with the Bar Association, ma'am, most of them are out celebrating the appointment of one of their members to a federal judgeship."

"That would be Gilbert Montano?" she asked.

"Yes, ma'am, care to leave a message?"

Mrs. Pollifax sought wildly for a message that might sum up her past several days. "Tell him," she said carefully, "that his wife has been—has been called *away*. And that Mr. Carstairs—that's C-a-r-s-t-a-i-r-s—needs her a few days longer. Did I say that too fast for you?"

"No, ma'am, I've got it all down, shall I read it back?"

"Please do."

Once this had been accomplished she hung up and swallowed her disappointment at not reaching Cyrus. On the other hand, she reflected, he would probably have tried to reach *her* during the past several days and suffered the same disappointment, so it was only fair that she experience it, too. He would come home to an empty house—a house with bread crumbs and sardine tins in a closet, no wife, and possibly no car yet if Pete had not had time to retrieve it. She could only remind herself that in the refrigerator he would find salami and a chicken as well as the Garden Club sandwiches artistically arranged on a platter.

The Garden Club felt a very long time ago.

She stopped Bishop as he rushed through the office and asked for Willie's phone number in Maine and dialed it. He must have been sitting by his phone waiting for news, because he answered on the first ring. "Willie, it's Emmy Reed," she said. "How is Boozy Tim?"

Willie took his time answering. "I've been in touch, Emmy, he's coming out of it okay, but a real close call, believe me. Those two *bengs* nearly killed him with all that dope, and he's still pretty confused, but the doc's with him and he's had his stomach pumped out, poor guy. Jake and Pogo are with him, too."

"That's good news. It's tear-down night after you close, isn't it?"

"Yep—sorry you're missing it. By the way, you were suspicious about Lubo. The police made him talk. Insisted." Willie chuckled. "Seems he's a math whiz who started a computer company in the '80s—very big with Wall Street—and then Japanese competition drove him into bankruptcy and closed him up. The crazy guy decided to make a clean break and have some fun for a change."

"How very creative!" said Mrs. Pollifax.

"No, crazy." He laughed. "But I promised to tell you something, didn't I. About Anyeta Inglescu?"

"Yes—you *do* know of her?"

"Know of her? She's my grandmother. *Ja develesa,* Emmy," he said, and hung up.

On the flight to New Haven Mrs. Pollifax found herself once again yawning, and once again seated next to this engaging child whom she'd discovered in her closet, and she could not help but experience a slight sense of *déjà vu*. It seemed very strange to be traveling with Carstairs; he had not been exactly forthcoming, and she had no idea what had triggered this whole-hearted commitment to helping Kadi and her friend, not to mention his interest in Ubangiba; Bishop had said something about his being obsessed with the country for the past few days, but she had no idea why. Certainly *something* must be happening there, or else Carstairs had gone berserk but she was confident that Carstairs never went berserk.

At the police station Carstairs insisted upon a room in the rear of the building, well out of sight, and they were given one lined with lockers and with cartons piled high in one corner. Chairs were carried in, and Mrs. Pollifax and Kadi sat in a silence permeated by tension while Carstairs was summoned to the telephone a number of times, to return looking pleased.

He was with them again when there came sounds in the corridor of a voice protesting, other voices muffling the protest, the door was opened, and two policemen ushered in Sammat Yusufu. As the officers released him, Sammy's mouth dropped open at the sight of the three people waiting for him, and as Kadi rose from her chair he gasped, *"Kadi?"*

"Hi, Sammy," she said, beaming at him. "I think I've brought help."

Mrs. Pollifax decided that the snapshot she had seen of Sammy had not done him justice: he was full grown and mature now, the rich dark color of his skin set off by a white shirt open at the throat; his eyes were thoughtful under a slash of black brows, his features strong and well-cut . . . *the face of a poet or a prince,* thought Mrs. Pollifax, or, from the look of his broad shoulders, a boxer. But if her first impression was of a wary young man this had changed when he saw Kadi: his face lit up with pleasure, even joy, and he exuded warmth.

"But what can this mean?" he asked, his eyes moving from Kadi to Carstairs to Mrs. Pollifax.

Carstairs said, "It means, from what Kadi has told us, that we've needed a serious talk with you alone, and definitely without your roommate."

Sammat's face relaxed. "Without Clarence . . . I see. But this is very clever of you, those two policemen will tell you that Clarence insisted he come with me, it was necessary for them to physically push him away. Which was astonishing," he added frankly.

"Exactly, and we mustn't keep you long from him."

"Kadi did all this?" Sammat asked, turning to her.

"Well, you see, after seeing you on Monday I was followed," she explained, "and this is Mrs. Pollifax in whose house I hid for two days—to get away from them—and this is Mr. Carstairs, who is—"

Carstairs interrupted her curtly. "Who is a friend. Sammy, we'd like to know who sent you to the United States four years ago, and with Clarence Mulimo as a guard. Do sit!"

"I will stand, sir, because Clarence, he is under very strict orders and—"

"From whom?" snapped Carstairs.

"This I don't know, sir, and there has been no way

to find out. I felt at first that when they assassinated my father they would have killed me, too, if I didn't have some value for them in the future. I think they sent me here to get me out of the way, but lately this has changed. From what I've learned, eavesdropping on Clarence's phone calls—the phone is in the hall but near our room—I think something is going to happen soon in my country, a coup perhaps, I don't know, but I do think that soon I will be taken back to Ubangiba, possibly to be killed, or if there is a coup then to become—what is the word, sir, a puppet?"

"That will do," nodded Carstairs.

"Yes, puppet. To be shown to the people as their leader, because they respect the royal line, but with someone behind me pulling the strings."

"You don't know who that would be?"

He shook his head. "No, sir, but Clarence has had his suitcase packed for a week, and there have been phone calls to him every night, like never before. I thought he might have been told to—but this is the United States, he could not as easily kill me here. Sir, I really must return to my dorm or Clarence will become suspicious."

Carstairs said in a hard voice, "I can tell you why Clarence has had his bags packed for a week. The news came over the wire services last night that President Simoko is dead."

"Dead?" cried Kadi.

"*Heya,*" gasped Sammat, and then, "But he has been in good health, surely this means—"

Carstairs nodded. "Yes, of course. His death has to have been planned."

"Poison or a bullet?" asked Mrs. Pollifax with interest.

Carstairs gave her an amused glance. "We don't know yet, but since arriving in this room my assistant Bishop has telephoned to report that Sammat and Clarence Mulimo, and a Mr. Achille Lecler, are booked to fly to Paris tomorrow morning, and presumably from there to Ubangiba on the Monday morning flight 1192."

Sammat felt for a chair and sat down.

"Would you be a good leader?" asked Carstairs softly. "Would the people accept you?"

Kadi made a move to speak but Mrs. Pollifax shook her head.

"I have studied hard to be one—always hoping," Sammat said gravely, and suddenly looked much older. "I have majored in economics, I have studied the many agricultural experiments taking place in Africa, I have studied democratic systems, and banking. I believe the people would accept me, which would be most unfortunate if I cannot speak truth to them or make the changes needed to bring prosperity to my country."

"But you feel sure the people would accept you?" repeated Carstairs.

It was a question asked again but in a different voice, and Mrs. Pollifax gave him a quick, curious glance. Definitely there were undercurrents here of which she could only guess.

Kadi said, "Even if uncertain of who he is at first they would accept him because of—"

"You have it?" asked Sammat. When she nodded he smiled, and to Carstairs he said, "When my grandfather was dying, sir, he summoned the royal diviners—those he trusted to speak truth—and they threw the cowrie shells and told him they saw only evil for ten harvests, and that he must have his son—my father—bury the sacred royal gold ring and let no one see it for ten years, and no one know of this but my father. When my father became President, just before he was killed—as if he knew it would happen—he showed me where it was hidden."

Mrs. Pollifax looked at Kadi and smiled. "So that's what Sammy gave you in the coffee house. Under the table."

Kadi flushed.

Startled, Carstairs murmured, "I have read something of that sacred gold ring, yes. You mean you have it? Is it known that you have it?"

Sammat said gravely, "It is not known, sir, no. I have kept it carefully concealed."

Carstairs glanced at his watch and made a face. "You *must* be delivered back to your dormitory. The police will have found it a case of mistaken identity and will apologize formally in front of Clarence for bringing you here at such an hour. It also looks obvious that you will be flying to Paris tomorrow and then to Ubangiba."

Sammat stood and waited, his face expressionless. "It seems unbelievable, sir, but I don't see how—"

"You will not be alone," Carstairs told him. "In Paris when you board flight 1192 you will see me—my name is Carstairs—traveling with a Mrs. Reed and her daughter, who will be Kadi, as well as with two other gentlemen who will join us in Paris. Since Kadi is known to Clarence you will find her somewhat disguised but in any case you will give no sign of recognition or take any notice of us, you understand? *Not until we arrive in Ubangiba.*"

Puzzled, Sammat said, "I recognize you then, sir? But how could this be explained?"

"We need a connection." Carstairs turned to Kadi, "I understand that your father was a missionary in the country?"

She nodded warily.

"We'll use that," he said. "I will have visited her father some years ago—Kadi can fill me in on details. You were introduced to me then, and having suddenly recognized me you will introduce yourself and invite us all to go with you."

Sammat said dryly, "Even to prison if that is what they plan for me? I have, after all, been something of a prisoner already these past few years."

Carstairs smiled. "I would think it more likely the President's palace, but let's just say that I want to be certain no one disposes of you as they did the late President Simoko."

It was very warm in the room but Mrs. Pollifax shivered at this.

"So—off you go," Carstairs said abruptly, and

opened the door to the hall. To the two men outside he said, "You can return him now."

Kadi said, "The ring's in my knapsack, Sammy, hidden in the lining. Would you like it now?"

"No, Kadi," he said, smiling. "Keep it for me—until we reach home."

Sammy walked out, joined at once by the pair of men who had brought him there, and Carstairs glanced again at his watch. "You were right, Kadi, your young friend's in considerable danger. Back to headquarters now, to wrap things up and get a few hours' sleep—Bishop will have booked rooms for you—and then—"

"And then?" asked Mrs. Pollifax.

"At eight tomorrow morning we fly to Paris—on another airline, of course—to await Monday morning's flight to Ubangiba."

CHAPTER 18

IT WAS IN PARIS THAT MRS. POLLIFAX AT last reached Cyrus in Connecticut. "You're home!" she exclaimed. "I was afraid I'd miss you."

"I'm home but the house is damn empty," he growled. "What the devil are you doing in Paris?"

"I'm quite safe, I'm with Carstairs."

"Carstairs! Thought he never left his desk."

"He said it was high time he did."

"How long have you been in Paris? When did he call you in?"

"He didn't, this time I called *him*. Or Bishop," she amended. "On Wednesday night. Possibly you haven't been home long enough to notice the empty sardine tins and crumbs in the closet, and the car missing?"

"So that's it," Cyrus said. "Car's not missing. Struck me as damn odd, though. Just paid off the taxi on arrival when a man drives our car up the driveway here, hands me the keys and goes off in the taxi I came in. Didn't *look* like a mechanic."

"I doubt that he was," Mrs. Pollifax told him frankly, "since I had to abandon the car in Worcester, Massachusetts."

"Worcester! Emily, what in the world—"

"Cyrus, I'll explain later, it's nearly time for the plane. I expect truly to be home in two or three days and—I must run—see you soon!"

She hung up quickly before he could ask what plane she was about to board. This was a pity, she thought, because Cyrus was probably the one person in fifty who would have heard of Ubangiba and who would know precisely where it was located on the continent of Africa. Replacing the phone in its cradle she glanced toward Gate 12, where a line was already gathering for the twice-weekly departure for Languka, Ubangiba. Seeing Kadi she smiled; *poor Kadi,* she thought, masquerading in a blonde wig with corkscrew curls like Shannon's and inhabiting a noisy yellow dress, her eyes concealed behind huge purple-rimmed dark glasses. Carstairs stood behind her with the stranger who had joined them at the hotel after breakfast, and who had been introduced as John Stover.

This is Carstairs's ballgame now, she thought, and

admitted that at first she had minded very much his being so secretive about his intentions. She found that it no longer mattered now what he was up to, he was giving her the opportunity to observe a real professional at work, a man who had been OSS-trained in World War II and had operated in the Paris underground and later in Libya. She had admired his original bent of mind ever since she'd met him, and now she intended to watch and learn. *Watch closely,* she resolved, and as she observed Carstairs from this distance she already noticed something strange take place: Carstairs had brought with him on the flight to Paris a brown leather attaché case; now she saw a man at the rear of the line move up to Carstairs, stand beside him for a moment, and without looking at him place a black alligator-hide attaché case on the floor next to Carstairs, and carry away Carstairs's brown one.

So now Carstairs had a black attaché case, and a very elegant one, too, which must be important. *Beautifully done,* she thought admiringly, *but certainly mysterious.*

Moving her gaze to the head of the line she caught a glimpse of Sammat, now wearing a bright *dashiki,* and she wondered which of the men near him was the Mr. Lecler with whom he was to travel, and whether he was really named Lecler at all, and if he was as French as his name sounded. *An extremely interesting trip,* she mused, and leaving the bank of phones she walked over to join Carstairs, Kadi, and Mr. Stover.

Once on the plane she sat next to Kadi, with Carstairs in a seat behind them; when she turned to speak to him she saw that his seat companion was the man who had traded attaché cases with him. They were introducing themselves now, as if they were strangers to each other, the man explaining that his name was Devereaux, he was a Parisian, and then he and Carstairs began speaking in French and she could no longer eavesdrop—which of course was why they were speaking French, she reminded herself. Definitely, she thought, the attaché case needed keeping an eye on, in case any more conjuring tricks took place in Languka.

The plane was only half-filled: Sammat's party had vanished into first class; Kadi explained that the groups of businessmen on the plane would probably stay just the night and one day in Languka, because on the following day a local plane from Agadez would land in Languka on its way to Dakar. Kadi thought the two stewardesses were Hausa and Fulani, and the steward Ethiopian but she couldn't speak to them because she was traveling incognito. This she mentioned regretfully before she drew out a book from her knapsack: Camus's *The Plague.* Mrs. Pollifax, who had left home on Wednesday with only a purse, was reduced to magazines bought in Paris.

Four hours later they began their descent over Ubangiba and Mrs. Pollifax looked down at a desert that was dotted with small moving objects that she guessed to be goats or cattle; soon the desert changed into green fields, and then brown fields threaded by a single dirt road, with occasional villages of conical huts. These were followed by clusters of shanties, then a suburb of square white concrete houses, and then a broad tree-lined boulevard marking Languka itself, which was a dusty-looking, crowded city of flat low buildings, except for two colonial-style white buildings with sloping roofs. "Palaces," said Kadi scornfully, looking over Mrs. Pollifax's shoulder as the plane swept low over the city and continued beyond it to the airport. "President Daniel Simoko Airport," announced the pilot, and they landed bumpily.

And so, thought Mrs. Pollifax, *we are here, and I have no idea why, unless it's to be sure that Sammat isn't murdered or sent to prison, but I can't believe the CIA to be THAT altruistic.* She rose and followed Kadi down the aisle, with Carstairs and Devereaux behind her. A platform was wheeled up to the door of the plane and they descended into an almost suffocating heat and sun to walk toward a gleaming white terminal building with a photograph of the President over the entrance. Mr. Devereaux hurried past her and she saw that it was he who now carried the black attaché case that he had presented to Carstairs in Paris. He passed Sammat and Clarence and the man at their side who had to be Mr. Achille Lecler. In one quick glance of appraisal Mrs. Pollifax received the impression that Mr. Lecler was a man of great efficiency, this from the manner in which he herded his two charges along, his lips thinned with impatience, but a man who also enjoyed his luxuries and was somewhat vain, as witness the strip of mustache punctuating his pale face, the cream-colored silk suit that he wore, and the black-and-white shoes with pointed toes. Except for the air of arrogance that he'd cultivated, she thought he looked simply a nondescript middle-aged white man struggling against a growing paunch from too rich a diet, and given to inappropriate clothes. Certainly he looked out of place in Ubangiba.

Mr. Devereaux, leading the crowd to Passport Control, moved through it quickly with a nod to the cluster of uniformed policemen, slowed, and then reached Customs only a little ahead of Sammat's group. Both his carry-on bag and his attaché case were opened and Mrs. Pollifax observed their contents: pajamas, shirts, toilet articles, and books. Mr. Lecler was next in line, and it appeared that he too carried a black attaché case fashioned out of the hide of an alligator, a fact that she'd not noticed as he disembarked. His case, however, was not opened. Instead he was greeted with a polite nod by the Customs officer and his attaché case was merely placed on the conveyor belt to be carried through the metal detector.

They know him here, realized Mrs. Pollifax, and having promised herself that she would keep an eye on all such attachés she was now rewarded, although it remained difficult to believe what she saw: for just one second Mr. Devereaux's and Mr. Lecler's matching cases lay on the Customs counter, and having diligently kept Mr. Devereaux's—or Carstairs's—in view, she was stunned to note—could her eyes be deceiving her?—that Mr. Devereaux walked away with Mr. Lecler's black attaché case. *More* sleight of hand! She hastily dropped her gaze, and with both men gone she deposited her purse on the counter.

"This is all?" said the man.

"It's a large purse," she pointed out as he drew from it the pajamas she'd had to buy in Paris, followed by brush, comb, lipstick, toothbrush, and wallet.

He gave her a disapproving glance and allowed her to move toward the exit.

It was now that she heard Sammat say, "But—excuse me, sir, are you not the Mr. Carstairs who once visited Mr. Hopkirk, the mission doctor here?"

She turned to see Carstairs react warmly. "You're not—you can't be—Kadi's friend Sammy? We met, yes—how many years ago? But this is astonishing!"

"Isn't it?" said Sammat, glowing securely now as he shook hands with him. "I return, sir, from university in the United States after four years away from my country."

"No!" cried Carstairs in surprise. "Four years! But I must introduce you to my sister Mrs. Reed-Pollifax and her daughter Katherine, and this is my friend John Stover, an anthropologist, and there is one more to our party but I see he has gone ahead. My dear Sammy, we simply *cannot* part now, after all these years. I remember so well what a good time we had!"

"Indeed we mustn't, no," Sammy said, looking

suddenly mischievous. "We are heading for the palace, which I'm sure you would enjoy very much seeing. It is quite new and most lavish, I hear. May I introduce Clarence Mulimo and Mr. Achille Lecler with whom I traveled? I'm sure they would like you to see the palace, too." He darted a quick glance at Mr. Lecler, whose lips had contracted into such a thin line that he appeared almost lipless; definitely he did not appreciate Sammat's offer of hospitality. "And you must also be in need of refreshment after the long flight."

Kadi said in a gushing voice, "Oh, I would *love* to see a palace. A real palace? Mums, did you hear what he said? A real palace, wouldn't it be *thrilling*?"

Carstairs gave her a startled glance, smiled faintly, and returned his gaze to Sammat, saying politely, "If it's not an intrusion—?"

Mr. Lecler said with equal politeness, "It is a most *inconvenient* time, perhaps tomorrow? There is a reception committee waiting outside, and Sammat is to be presented to the people in only an hour—"

"Which I'm sure Mr. Carstairs would enjoy seeing, too," said Sammy firmly, and to Mrs. Pollifax, not looking at Kadi, he explained, "It seems that my homecoming has been known for some hours, and the people told that I am returning, our President having died only Friday."

Carstairs said in surprise, "But I had forgotten, Sammy, you are King Zammat's grandson!" and to

Mrs. Pollifax, "This will be exciting indeed, Sammy being a member of royalty."

"Royalty!" squealed Kadi, clapping her hands girlishly. "Oh just wait 'til I tell all the kids at home!"

Sammat smothered a laugh. "Quite so," he said, and ignoring Mr. Lecler he said regally, "You have a car outside? We will leave together."

"But Sammat—"

"We go together," Sammy told Mr. Lecler sternly. "He is a *friend*, you wish me to be miserly? One *shares* with a friend."

"I do not like this," said Mr. Lecler warningly, and Mrs. Pollifax observed from the expression on his face that Mr. Lecler could also be ruthless as well as arrogant.

Sammat turned his back on him to walk beside Carstairs, saying, "How many years has it been, sir?"

"Too many! Ah, Devereaux, here you are. . . . We've been invited to the palace, and this is the old friend of the Hopkirks' about whom I was telling you. Sammy, this is Monsieur Devereaux."

Clarence Mulimo had disappeared; Mr. Lecler was clearly outnumbered. They moved in a group toward the brilliant sunshine just beyond the arched entrance, over which hung still another huge photograph with SIMOKO in blazing red letters. Mrs. Pollifax noted that Mr. Lecler gave Carstairs several quick, puzzled glances. Perhaps there was suspicion in his gaze, too, as there very well might be, she reflected, should this man have had anything to do with Chigi Scap Metal and its pursuit of Kadi. Certainly he had taken charge of Sammy and Clarence, there was no doubt about that.

The reception committee of which he had spoken was waiting outside, although Mrs. Pollifax had never before seen such a sullen-looking group of people, kept firmly in place by scarlet-coated policemen; it seemed obvious they had been rounded up unwillingly for this event.

Sammat, scrutinizing the faces behind the ropes, gave a cry of "Laraba!" He broke away to stride toward a thin, barefooted woman wearing a red T-shirt, long black skirt, and polka-dotted kerchief. Her closed dark face came to life, she laughed, and they embraced.

With a sigh Kadi said, "Damn, I'd like to hug her, too, that's Laraba and here I am all gussied up as a blonde in weird clothes."

"A good friend?"

"A *very* good friend, it was she and Rakia, my father's nurse, who hid me and smuggled me out of Ubangiba."

The sullen faces in the crowd became less sullen; a few men broke ranks to crowd around Sammat and shake his hand, and then Mr. Lecler irritably pointed out that a limousine was waiting. He missed one detail, however: as Sammat returned to them he grinned at Kadi, and in passing said to her softly, "Laraba says hello and welcome, she wasn't fooled for a minute."

Kadi laughed.

The grass surrounding the terminal looked a hectic green, like Astro-turf, and the long white limousine incongruous among the battered cars and taxis parked near the entrance. *What a curious group we are,* thought Mrs. Pollifax; Stover and Devereaux poker-faced, Lecler furious, Kadi and Sammat beaming at each other, and who knew what Carstairs was thinking or feeling? Reaching the limousine it proved difficult to arrange the seating: eventually Mr. Stover volunteered to sit beside the driver but Mr. Lecler was forced to employ a jump seat, obviously resenting this very much.

As they left the airport behind, Mrs. Pollifax thought that once there must have been a grand design for the approach to the city, because this was the tree-lined boulevard that she had seen from the plane, running in a straight line from airport to palace; unfortunately, years of neglect, coups, and riots had dissipated any grandeur. The parade of dusty trees barely screened the hovels behind them, and the walls of once-prosperous villas were pocked with bullet holes. When the walls ended there was an eruption of colorful, less private life: a crowded marketplace with signs in startling neon shades proclaiming FODIA! COLA! MKATE! MAKALA! CAFÉ!—at which point it became necessary to stop and allow a herd of goats to cross the boulevard.

"Now as to the program for the rest of the day," said Mr. Lecler, leaning forward in his jump seat to claim Sammat's attention. "Within the hour there will be a spontaneous gathering of the people outside the palace to welcome you, and you will speak to them graciously from the balcony. There is then the

President's funeral already being planned, elaborate, of course, and as impressive as our President Simoko's years of rule have been. Later there will be a meeting with the chiefs of the Shambi and Soto tribes to discuss the next government." With a small tight smile he added, "And I have already assured you that we will find *something* for you to do in that government, after which there will be a state dinner in the Gold Room."

Mrs. Pollifax, seated beside Sammat, heard him mutter words in a low voice. Silent until now he said, "*Trɔbul de taym in nɔ dé.*"

Only Kadi, seated on the other side of him, understood that in pidgin English he was saying there was a lot of trouble here.

Mrs. Pollifax only heard her murmur, "That's for sure, *bo*."

CHAPTER 19

THE APPROACH TO THE PALACE WAS LINED with bougainvillea, and then the limousine swept up to an entrance that would surely equal the most luxurious of European hotels, its doors manned by guards in uniform.

Sammat said calmly, "As you will recall, Mr. Carstairs, my grandfather did not live in a palace but in a house made of earth in the royal compound."

Carstairs said quickly, "I remember, yes."

The guards snapped to attention as the limousine stopped, and one of them came forward to open the car's doors. "Ah, Mr. Lecler," he said, and saluted.

So he really is well known, thought Mrs. Pollifax, making note of this, *and perhaps even lives here?*

They were escorted through heavy glass doors into

a vast entrance hall of marble, at the end of which hung a gold relief of President Simoko's smiling face. Carstairs, looking around, murmured, "The President did himself well."

"It would make an excellent hospital or school," pointed out Sammat.

Lecler, overhearing this, laughed. "I don't think we'd agree on *that*." To the guard he said, "Joseph, take these people to the Ceremonial Hall," and to Sammat, "And you—you will come to my office, please."

Sammat smiled politely. "I will first see my friends to the hall you speak of," and to Joseph, "I am Sammat Yusufu, and do not know where the Ceremonial Hall is, will you show us? And bring my guests some cold drinks to refresh them."

The guard's eyes widened. "You—*you* are Zammat—of *Zammat zisanu ndi zitato*?" He bowed low.

Sammy placed a hand on his arm. "Only the grandchild—*mdzukulu*—of a King, Joseph. No need to bow, just show us the way."

"Yes, *sir*!"

Mr. Lecler looked very nearly apoplectic, but hid it by abruptly turning away to stride toward a gilt door on the left; he opened it and vanished, presumably into an office.

Joseph led the way up the broad marble staircase, speaking with animation to Sammat in their own language; as Mrs. Pollifax climbed the stairs, Carstairs caught up with her to say pleasantly, sotto voce, "No way to bring weapons into the country, Mrs. P, we may have to rely on Stover's judo, and you and your brown belt you-know-what. *Be vigilant.*" Having said this he accelerated his pace and moved ahead to join John Stover.

So, thought Mrs. Pollifax, *something is going to happen,* and she felt reinvigorated.

Reaching the second floor, they followed Joseph across a wide corridor to a pair of gleaming brass doors that Joseph dramatically swung open for them. Here Mrs. Pollifax stopped, frankly awed by what she saw: a huge room with polished mahogany floors, the right wall lined with french windows opening onto a balcony, and a ceiling that glittered with crystal chandeliers. . . . A few steps into the room and her gaze included clusters of gilt chairs with scarlet upholstered seats, and at the far end what looked like a throne. Certainly it was the focal point of the room, a heavy golden stool—surely gold, not gilt—placed squarely against a scarlet tapestry on which two serpents were prominent. On either side of the throne hung matching scarlet curtains on long rods, and Mrs. Pollifax watched with interest as John Stover immediately crossed the room to the curtain on the right and flung it open to reveal a narrow hallway beyond; with a nod to Carstairs he closed the curtain, walked to the other side of the throne and repeated his performance before joining them again.

Seeing Mrs. Pollifax watch him, he smiled and said lightly, "Just curiosity."

Amused, Mrs. Pollifax thought, *Oh really?*

No one spoke. Devereaux strolled over to the french doors, opened one, and stepped out on the balcony to return, saying, "Already a crowd of people milling around."

"Herded here by the police?" said Sammat dryly.

Devereaux shook his head. "Saw no police."

They turned as the brass doors opened and Joseph arrived carrying a tray holding glasses and a pitcher; an aide followed with a table on which Joseph placed the tray, and then Lecler walked in; at once Mrs. Pollifax felt the change and knew this was what they'd been waiting for. Lecler still carried his black attaché case but now in his other hand he held a sheaf of papers.

"So," he said almost benevolently, "you have refreshments and the people are gathering below. Sammat, it is nearly time."

"A beautiful room," Mrs. Pollifax told him. "That lovely gold bench or stool, for instance—" She turned to point, but her glance abruptly slid instead to the scarlet curtain on the right of the throne: it lacked several inches in length so that it did not quite meet the floor and she saw that someone was now standing behind it, listening.

"—solid gold," Lecler was saying. "It has belonged to the Kings of Ubangiba for centuries."

No one else had turned to look toward the throne. "Surely 18-karat gold?" she suggested, and inched her way toward Carstairs to nudge him. Without moving her lips she murmured, "Someone's hiding behind the curtain."

"Eighteen karat?" scoffed Lecler. "Absolutely not, it is 24-karat gold."

Her nudge and her words produced in Carstairs no glance toward the curtained alcove; he merely looked amused and nodded.

"So," repeated Mr. Lecler, ending his attempt at hostlike graciousness, "it grows time now, Sammat." To Carstairs he said, "You comprehend, he has a speech to make? He must studiously read it to be sure that he does not stumble over any words."

Carstairs said, "Yes, it sounds as if they're eager to see and hear you, Sammat, you mustn't keep them waiting."

"No, no," Lecler said quickly, "you do not understand. He does not speak *yet*, he has not seen the speech written for him. Joseph, escort these guests to the Green Room . . . Sammat," he said, handing him the sheaf of papers, "read over your speech now to be sure it goes smoothly."

Carstairs stepped forward, took the papers from Sammat, and tore them into shreds. As they floated to the floor like confetti he said curtly, "I think Sammat knows what he wishes to say without needing someone else's words put into his mouth."

Lecler stared at him incredulously. "You dare?" he gasped. "You *dare*? Sir, you have just destroyed the speech that Sammat, a King's grandson, is to make to his people! Such impertinence, such interference, is intolerable. One call to the guards, Mr. Carstairs, and you will find our prisons very unpleasant!"

"I'm sure they are," agreed Carstairs, "but you might first like to know what brings me here to this country."

"*Not* a tourist?" scoffed Lecler angrily.

"*Not* a tourist, no," said Carstairs, and added casually, "I have merely been following to Ubangiba fifty million dollars in ransom money picked up three mornings ago in Westchester County in the United States."

A stunned silence followed until Carstairs broke it to add pleasantly, "Of course Ubangiba will be very grateful for the fifty million dollars in unmarked bills that you've brought into the country, and which you no doubt *believe* you have in that black attaché case on the floor beside you." As Lecler looked down at his case in horror Carstairs said in a kind voice, "I don't think you'll find the fifty million there, Lecler. You will note that I, too, have a black attaché case, and my friend Devereaux, a most gifted practitioner of sleight of hand, produced miracles as you both passed through Customs. I will not tell you anything more about him but I will add that Mr. Stover is not an anthropologist but a member of the United States FBI."

Wonderful, thought Mrs. Pollifax.

Lecler gaped at Carstairs and then with trembling hands tried to open the catch on his attaché case, forgetting that it was locked.

Mrs. Pollifax, daring to speak, asked, "Does this have something to do with—"

Carstairs interrupted her to say, "Sammat, go to the balcony now, the crowds sound restive, they want you."

"But sir—"

"It's best you go, Sammat."

"But sir—"

"Now," Carstairs told him flatly.

Sammat walked to the french doors, opened them, turned once to look back at them all, then walked out onto the balcony to a roar of sound that was deafening. Kadi walked to the doors and closed them.

"Open your attaché case," Carstairs told Lecler.

"No," snapped Lecler, "and I don't know what you're talking about." He drew himself erect. "In the meantime," he said harshly, accusingly, "you provoke an international incident with such insolence, you have come here—an *American*—to illegally and illicitly disrupt the affairs of the sovereign government of Ubangiba. The police must be called. Joseph—at once!"

"On the contrary," Carstairs told him, "I didn't come for that purpose at all. I followed a ransom, it's true, but that's not what personally brought me here. What I came for—" He turned toward the curtained alcove and said, "You can come out now, Bidwell." And to Lecler he said, "Bidwell is what I came for."

"Bidwell?" faltered Mrs. Pollifax. "Henry Bidwell?"

From the other side of the room Kadi gasped, "The man held hostage in New York? The kidnapped man?"

"Neither hostage nor kidnapped," said Carstairs. "Well, Bidwell?"

The curtain trembled a little but did not open. It was Mrs. Pollifax who walked the few paces across the room to pull the curtain aside and stand there staring at the same thin, autocratic face she had seen pictured in newspapers and on television, but now drained of color, bloodless and stricken. Turning to Carstairs she said, bewildered, "But how—and *here*?"

"Don't move, any of you," Lecler said in a deadly calm voice. "Don't move, I have a gun. Mr. Carstairs, you will kindly slide your attaché case across the floor to me, *now*, at once!"

Carstairs hesitated and then, with one foot, pushed his attaché case several feet across the polished floor as Lecler drew from his cream-colored silk suit a gun that Mrs. Pollifax automatically identified as a 9mm Smith and Wesson.

"None of you," said Lecler, "will leave this room alive."

Oh dear God, thought Mrs. Pollifax, *I was counted on to help and now I'm too far away, and that means Stover—Stover, if you know judo, use it NOW.*

But it was Joseph in his scarlet uniform who moved up behind Lecler as soundlessly as a cat and sent the man stumbling forward, grabbed him before he fell, turned him around and hit him hard and furiously across his jaw, knocking him to the floor with his fists. *"Udiyo,"* he cried passionately. *"Udiyo, udiyo . . . Be ku-bada udiyo."*

From the other side of the room Kadi called, "He is calling him evil—*evil*—born to be evil."

Joseph stood defiantly, breathing hard. Carstairs said gravely, "And we thank you, Joseph, for our lives." Leaning over he picked up Lecler's gun and training it on the man framed by the scarlet curtains he said, "Well, Bidwell? What do you have to say for yourself, and to the millions of people—not to mention your wife and children—who have pictured you kidnapped, bound and gagged and abused in some basement cellar for ten days, doubtless even praying for you? You have demeaned and insulted every hostage that's ever been taken captive and who has lived with *real* terror."

Bidwell stammered, "I . . . I . . ." and he fainted, sinking to the floor with one of his outflung arms resting on Mrs. Pollifax's shoe. With distaste she withdrew her foot and walked around him. "*Not* a hostage?" she said.

"As pretty a disappearing act as you'll see in your lifetime," said Carstairs.

Kadi had opened the door to the balcony and Mrs. Pollifax could hear Sammat's voice clearly and confidently speaking to the people in their language. "But how did you know?" Mrs. Pollifax asked Carstairs.

From the crowds outside came a roar of laughter and then a cheer, and Kadi turned to them, smiling.

"Sammy has told them *everything*," she said "and they are *with* him, they understand what nearly happened, and he makes a promise to them of *makasi*—a new path. You heard, Joseph? *Makasi!*"

CHAPTER 20

IT WAS EVENING IN THE PALACE. SAMMAT had met with the Chiefs of the Shambi and the Soto, and had gravely accepted their plea that he take over the *ufumo*—the chieftainship—of their sorrowing country and restore its heart, or *mtima*. Stover and Devereaux had vanished to make a number of phone calls, Devereaux to Paris and Stover to Washington—a laborious and time-consuming process—while Achille Lecler was under guard in a clinic awaiting a doctor to wire his jaw. Following a brilliant sunset, night had fallen like a curtain, but the darkness was filled with the muted sound of beating drums—talking drums, Sammy had told them, spreading news of the events of this day across the fields and the desert—*and now I know I really am in Africa,* thought Mrs. Pollifax.

She glowed with contentment: there had been a bath in a real tub—she had missed that at Willie's—and she had been loaned a *dashiki* while her clothes were being laundered and pressed. She was in Africa, of all places, witnessing the unmasking of a clever and unscrupulous billionaire; during the past several days she and Kadi had inadvertently arrived on the periphery of Carstairs's suspicions about Bidwell and the two of them had supplied him with the dimensions needed to confirm his suspicions. Two paths had converged: Carstairs had found his man and, what was most important to her young friend Kadi, they had brought Sammy safely home.

Yet only seven days ago, she remembered, she had neither heard of Sammy, nor of Ubangiba, nor of Kadi Hopkirk, who had been hiding for a day and a night in her hall closet. *Really,* she thought, *it has been QUITE an astonishing week!*

Now she presided over a long and candle-lit refectory table in the shadowy dining hall of the palace, Sammy and Kadi on either side of her, and Carstairs seated next to Bidwell, whose left hand was handcuffed to his chair.

"Well?" she said, addressing Carstairs across the table.

Carstairs gave her a faint smile and nodded. "Yes," he said, and turning to Bidwell, "You understand that we are your first judge and jury."

Bidwell licked dry lips and whispered, "But how

did you know? How did you ever guess? It was so carefully, so *very* carefully—"

"Planned, yes," agreed Carstairs. "For years, I'm sure."

"But—how? We made no mistakes, I *swear*."

Carstairs considered this judiciously. "I'd say that your worst miscalculation was insisting that you not know when or how your abduction was to take place, or by whom, leaving it entirely up to your two confederates, Lecler and Romanovitch, to arrange. Due, no doubt—I can only guess—to your fear of the abduction being witnessed. They were to do the dirty work, and you were to play the part of innocent victim, it had to look absolutely authentic should anyone chance to notice the abduction taking place. And so—not knowing precisely when or how—you left behind your engagement calendar locked in a drawer, a fact known only to your secretary who spoke of it to the FBI."

"Damn it," whispered Bidwell. "Damn *her*."

"And in that engagement calender were those five mysterious flight 1192's," continued Carstairs, ignoring this crude dismissal of a loyal secretary. "There were also, of course, your appointments with Desforges, Lecler, and Romanovitch, but it was the 1192's that piqued my curiosity. You were a man whose life appeared to be an open book and yet you made five mysterious and concealed trips to Ubangiba, and I might add that your Claiborne-Osborne people, when questioned, scarcely knew of the country's existence. Initially I felt those trips might hold the key to your abduction: a terrorist group, perhaps, or a band of Ubangiban nationalists who objected to your presence. I thought you might have been snatched by a group like that."

"But this scarcely—"

"Very true," agreed Carstairs. "Actually it was something that Desforges said—oh yes, I spoke with him in Rouen, he was very discreet, very proper, he refused to tell me anything except that you'd bought the mineral rights to the country. He did concede, however, that what had been discovered would be only modestly profitable, and he used a curious word: only with cheap, very cheap labor, he said. Very Leopoldish."

"Leopold?" repeated Sammat, startled.

"Yes, a name that I overlooked at the time; I was too disillusioned when our Geology Department reported that coal was the only possibility in Ubangiba, given the terrain. I had expected gold, or natural gas. . . . Perhaps it began when I asked myself why this passionate interest in coal? From you, a man accustomed to million-dollar deals, a man believed to be a billionaire; I very nearly lost interest."

"But you didn't," said Mrs. Pollifax, smiling.

He smiled back at her. "No, because at that point Bishop handed over to me his taped phone interview with you, Mrs. P, where you spoke of being chased through Connecticut and into Massachusetts by a van with 'Chigi Scap Metal' on its panels, and only an hour earlier that same van had been described to us by one of our men named Lazlo—but I won't bore you with that detail just now."

"Later?" urged Mrs. Pollifax, the name Lazlo being all too familiar to her.

"Later, yes. Suffice to say, it was at this point that Kadi and Mrs. Pollifax entered the picture. This Kadi," he said, smiling at her, "who grew up in Ubangiba, met a good friend in New Haven named Sammy who was also from Ubangiba, and who appeared to be in trouble. That's when political possibilities entered this puzzle to enhance matters, and of course very soon a most intriguing connection was made."

He met Bidwell's glance and held it. "Stop me if I'm wrong but I assume—having seen and heard your impassioned plea on video only Friday—that as soon as the abduction took place you were rushed somewhere to film several dramatic appeals to be issued at suitable intervals, and then—even before a ransom note was sent out—you were on your way to Ubangiba with a new passport. Of course you left Lecler in charge of the two Chigi Scap Metal chaps, and as you must know by now they were killed on Friday by Lecler, about the same time that President Simoko here in Ubangiba was murdered by Romanovitch."

"Who is still missing," Kadi reminded him.

"Not for long," said Carstairs. "Joseph has taken a few trusted friends in the police to look for him."

Sammat interrupted to say, "Joseph has also taken me to the room where President Simoko slept, sir, and has shown me the trunks of gold bullion hidden there . . . so much! It will certainly serve to back our currency, the *gwar* that has lost so much value. But how greedy Simoko was!"

"Bidwell was greedy, too," said Carstairs looking at him. "Fifty million ransom, Bidwell? *That* was rather suspicious. . . . My last-minute inquiries uncovered the fact that you'd never kept all your money in the United States—doubtless it was stashed away in Swiss banks—but it wasn't enough, you also wanted everything that remained in the United States, you wanted it *very* much, and what better way to get it moved out of the country than to be abducted and the ransom collected by Lecler and brought to Ubangiba."

Mrs. Pollifax, puzzled, said, "But why and for what?"

"Ah," said Carstairs, "that's where Leopold comes in. Look at Sammat, he knows what I mean."

Sammat nodded. "King Leopold and the Congo."

"Your question, Mrs. P, is the same question that I asked of myself: why and for what? A modest vein of coal certainly couldn't explain Bidwell's interest in the country. What then, I wondered, could it be? Having made billions and become sated with money, what did he still lack?"

They waited expectantly.

"I realized I was thinking too small. What he wanted was to own a country. His *own* country."

"Nobody can own a country," said Kadi flatly.

"No? King Leopold the Second did, and I'm sure

Bidwell had him in mind. . . . But let me tell you about King Leopold the Second of Belgium, who died in 1909. I've read and reread the story these past two days until I believe I can quote from memory." Leaning back in his chair he closed his eyes, and as if the pages had become engraved there he recited, " 'Failing to interest his country in acquiring the Congo during the "great scramble" for Africa during the late eighteen hundreds, the King used his own personal fortune to further his personal ambitions . . .' "

He opened his eyes to say in a harsh voice, "So he employed Henry Morton Stanley—you could almost substitute Lecler and Romanovitch here—to explore the Congo, to make treaties with the chiefs, and to map its rivers. Eventually Leopold established a trading monopoly in rubber from which he alone—not Belgium—made enormous profits under a system of abusive forced labor and sickening atrocities.

"And not until 1904," he continued, "did Europe wake up to the fact that a single individual owned an entire country—think of it, an entire country owned by one man—who ruled it as the most absolute of absolute monarchs."

"Owned a country!" whispered Kadi.

"Fair and square," nodded Carstairs. "And even when Europe learned of it—among other things, Conrad's *Heart of Darkness* brought it clearly to the world—Europe did nothing, nothing at all, being too occupied with its own small wars and conflicts."

"Wow," Kadi said, "I didn't know *that*."

"I did," Sammat said. "It was a bloody and brutal story in Africa's history."

"Well, Bidwell, am I right?" Carstairs asked, turning to him. "You intended to become the missing Judge Crater of this continent and rule a country using young Sammat as a decoration and ruling him as well, isn't this true? A new hobby, right? A toy to play with? A little fun for you in your later years?"

"Stop—stop," groaned Bidwell. "Tell me, I beg of you, what will happen to me now."

" 'Beg of' me?" mocked Carstairs. "Well, there are certain possibilities I can think of. . . . I admit, much to my sorrow, that at the moment I can think of no laws you've broken, unless as an accessory to the murder of President Simoko. Definitely, however, the fifty million dollars in ransom that you went to so much trouble to bring here—" He reached down for his attaché case and slid it across the table to Sammat. "I think it only fair and just that it remain in Ubangiba for the development of the country, since it was for that purpose it came here."

Bidwell made a strangled sound of protest.

"After all," pointed out Carstairs, "it's Bidwell money, originally a ransom to be paid to return you to the family that you've abandoned. That *could* be your future. Stover is conferring about that."

"Returned?" Bidwell said in a shocked voice. "To my family?"

Carstairs shrugged. "Why not? The ransom has been paid and will never be traced—those unmarked bills—and it's possible our government may think the most creative punishment is that you be found gagged and bound in New York and quietly returned to that family. With the stipulation, of course, that you immediately retire from Claiborne-Osborne International and never leave the United States or be involved in any business again."

"That fifty million is *mine*," Bidwell said desperately. "And you can't arrest me, you have no legal rights, we're on foreign soil!"

"Ah, but we're not arresting you," said Carstairs smoothly, "the FBI is only carrying out its assigned job of rescuing a kidnapped American citizen. We will merely be returning a captured American to the United States, where you may or may not be arrested. However, I would like to remind you that recently the Supreme Court ruled that in the case of 'hot pursuit' the FBI may enter a foreign country to recover a person wanted for criminal activities."

"I won't go," stormed Bidwell.

"Or," pointed out Carstairs, "the whole story can be told. The newspapers will love it, your family will be crushed, and I'm sure you can be sent to prison for *something*, I'm not sure for what, not being an expert on the subtleties of the law. If not as an accessory to murder, then surely Ubangiba can try you for the attempt to overthrow its government."

Bidwell attempted to rise from his chair but was held back by his handcuffs. "That's blackmail!" he shouted.

Carstairs laughed in his face.

They were silent, each of them staring at Bidwell

and realizing how very nearly he had succeeded in his scheme. It was only Carstairs, thought Mrs. Pollifax, who had been intuitive enough to weave together dissimilar and fragile threads to make a whole out of a crazy, outrageous pattern, and she marveled at him again.

The silence ended with a sigh as Carstairs said, "Enough . . . Stover is arranging a special plane for us in the morning—no rest for the weary!—to return Bidwell to the United States. Devereaux is going to stay on for a week, though, Sammat, and help in any way he can. I hope none of you feel we're deserting Sammat?"

"I'm a little tired," admitted Mrs. Pollifax. "Before I'm overwhelmed by jet lag I think I'd like to go home and see Cyrus."

"Kadi?"

Kadi said shyly, "Would it be possible for me to stay until the Thursday flight back to Paris and New York? I'd like to find my parents' graves—Laraba will know where. And visit with old friends."

"By all means," said Carstairs. "And Sammy? You'll be very busy, I'm thinking."

"I certainly will," he said earnestly. "We must restore the old legal system, once surviving lawyers can be released from prison. Banks and credit unions have to be opened again, and the Simoko army disbanded and new people trained. I'd like to turn half of this palace into an Agricultural Center, and half into a high school; but first I must bring in two experts whose books I have studied, they are agricultural experts on what can best be grown in Africa, and what experiments have been successful."

"And the fifty million dollars?" asked Mrs. Pollifax with a smile.

"Food," he said quickly. "Grain at *once* to fill the shops for the people to buy, and seeds—but the seeds will be given away. And yes, perhaps some equipment to mine that coal you spoke of, sir, so that it can fuel the digging of new wells—but I must go slowly and not make mistakes, sir."

"And elections?" asked Carstairs.

Sammat shook his head. "Not until the people have full bellies and a taste of what it feels like to be free. They would only vote for me now, you see, and that would be very bad."

Kadi grinned. "Well, if I learn you've made yourself President-for-Life, Sammy, I'll come over with my B-B gun and—"

"*Heya,* Kadi," he said, grinning, "you remember the time Duma shot wild by accident and—"

She giggled. "—and my father took six pellets out of me, and I couldn't sit down for a week."

Carstairs, watching them, smiled. "There is this, too, young lady. When you tire of art school—and if the CIA still exists," he added dryly, "we could use someone with your gift for sketching faces and remembering them."

"Well, thank you," she said, and to Mrs. Pollifax, "*Another* job offer, Emmy Reed!"

But Mrs. Pollifax was watching Carstairs, who was looking intently at each of their faces around the table. "It's extraordinary," he said. "We have here in this room, however briefly, all the characters who played out this drama. For me it's extraordinary."

"I don't suppose it happens often for you," conceded Mrs. Pollifax, "but this one you've seen through to the very end."

"No," said Sammat firmly, "he has seen it through to a *beginning*."

EPILOGUE

THIS WEEK WILLIE'S TRAVELING AMUSEMENT Shows were encamped not far from the ocean in southernmost Maine, so that on this early June morning the fragrance of salt air mingled companionably with the smell of the fresh sawdust that Jake was shoveling out of the truck being driven slowly around the midway. A morning breeze from the sea played with the seats of the ferris wheel and sent them swinging gently, while two seagulls observed the scene from the ridgepole of the Ten-in-One. The bright sun had not yet extinguished the shadows cast by the stalls but it picked out Shannon as she emerged from her trailer in a not-too-clean robe and made her way to the grab-joint. Down at his Spin the Wheel, Lubo had set up a laptop computer on the counter and was making calculations. In the trailer compound Gertie was hanging her washing out to dry, while three trailers beyond her the Snake Woman opened her door and sat down in the sun cradling a python in her arms.

It was an otherwise tranquil morning until its silence was suddenly invaded by the sound of the merry-go-round coming to life, its horses slowly rising and falling, its carousel bursting out with the lively rhythms of "Who Stole My Heart Away."

"Faster, Boozy Tim, or you'll rock us to sleep," called Cyrus, astride a black horse with a scarlet saddle.

"Yes, faster," called Mrs. Pollifax, and fluttered a hand at Kadi, who laughed up at them, paintbrush in one hand, a bucket of paint in the other, and who watched them as they rode side by side in perfect contentment, round and round, dreamily, and then the rollicking music paused, clicked and changed to "In the Good Old Summertime."

Kadi thought, *I have a family again*. . . .

Willie, striding onto the midway, came to an abrupt halt, startled by the sound of the carousel at such an early hour. He looked at Boozy Tim, and then at Cyrus and Mrs. Pollifax, and he shook his head and grinned. "Not *again*!" he said, and chuckled as he headed into the cook-house for coffee.

Discover—or rediscover—Dorothy Gilman's feisty grandmother and fearless CIA agent . . . Mrs. Pollifax!

THE UNEXPECTED MRS. POLLIFAX
THE AMAZING MRS. POLLIFAX
THE ELUSIVE MRS. POLLIFAX
A PALM FOR MRS. POLLIFAX
MRS. POLLIFAX ON SAFARI
MRS. POLLIFAX ON THE CHINA STATION
MRS. POLLIFAX AND THE HONG KONG BUDDHA
MRS. POLLIFAX AND THE GOLDEN TRIANGLE
MRS. POLLIFAX AND THE WHIRLING DERVISH
MRS. POLLIFAX AND THE SECOND THIEF
MRS. POLLIFAX PURSUED
MRS. POLLIFAX AND THE LION KILLER
MRS. POLLIFAX, INNOCENT TOURIST
MRS. POLLIFAX UNVEILED

Mrs. Pollifax's ex-CIA friend, Farrell, is heading to the Middle East on a personal mission—to retrieve the final manuscript of an Iraqi dissident novelist who was murdered in prison. Mrs. Pollifax is called upon to assist by acting like an innocent tourist in order to divert suspicion from Farrell's operation.

Soon the coils of Middle Eastern intrigue begin to unwind. Eluding their pursuers isn't easy, but Mrs. Pollifax takes her challenges straight up—and this one may be her stiffest yet. . . .